Wish Again

Deby Adair

The Unicorns of Wish Books

2

UnicornKisses

Australia

Faithfully dedicated to all creatures with hooves
With sincere love and gratitude to all my 'little unicorns.'
Immeasurably - for Legs - my own faithful Pud.

Cataloguing-in-Publication is held at the National Library of Australia

Adair, Deby
Wish Again
Revised ed.
ISBN: 978-0-9804513-1-3

First ed. published in 2011
Published in USA 2012
Revised ed. published by UnicornKisses 2019

Child and Youth Fiction

The Unicorns of Wish Books
②

Cover and Design by UnicornKisses Australia

Join us with other Kindred Spirits
www.unicornkisses.com

Contents

The Legend

Rising from the mists of sunset and reaching into dawn's surprise, there is a land called Wish. Guarded by ponds and watched by noble keepers, Wish awaits and prepares for adventures.

One day, a warrior dressed in splendid clothes, and handsome as he was rich, charged the shores of Wish. His desire was to slay a unicorn. He wanted the golden horn for its hidden powers and wisdom.

No matter how much he was told that a dead unicorn's horn was of no use to anyone, he would not listen and would not be told. He wasn't wanted in Wish and was heartily ignored, but the warrior returned again and again; he would not be swayed. It was his wish and his desire to have the horn of a unicorn. He promised a huge reward to those in the land.

But what did they care for bullion or gold? Would it make them strong? Give them wisdom? Teach them to be brave, kind, or fair?

There lived a sorcerer in Wish, and he too ignored the warrior's plea, but then one sad and foreboding night the sorcerer came forward with a changed mind. And so it was. The sorcerer told the warrior where he could find a unicorn and having done his duty he asked to have his gold, but the warrior was well studied and he knew the ancient lore... mighty unicorns would not appear for just anyone, so he ordered the sorcerer to bring a unicorn to him.

The sorcerer could have taken the gold and sent the warrior home; instead, using wild magic, he changed his appearance and shape to become the image of an innocent maiden.

He sat and waited when all his trickery was complete, on a boulder of a path well used. He held his breath and waited for a sacred unicorn. Meanwhile the warrior hid in bushes nearby, with his arrows and crossbow held ready, his handsome face excited and aglow!

Soon it happened. The wait was neither long nor hard before a pure white unicorn, with shy, soft steps, made herself known. Her breathtaking golden horn shone brightly as her gossamer mane and tail flowed in all their glory to the ground. With innocent eyes open and wide, the unicorn spoke like this: 'With your once kind heart now turned cold, would you sell your soul and kill virtue, for gold? You are not a maiden, so I offer you a chance: withdraw, send the warrior away and save yourself while you can.'

Discovered in his deception, the sorcerer was not humbled. He did not bow his head or beg forgiveness. Furiously he cast away his disguise, and with a twisted face, he cried out to the warrior.

Triumphant, the warrior shot the arrow from his bow with an aim that would surely make its mark, but the unicorn swiftly turned, so her shoulder was pierced and not her heart. She screamed, though, and to hear a unicorn scream is to hear the end of all that is fair.

The sound of her torment was heart-rending, desolate, a thing of dire anguish, and so it was that in that moment, the warrior knew what he had done. With blinding clarity he threw down his arrows and flung away his cruel crossbow, then ran in dread to fall at her feet.

'Forgive me,' he sobbed, 'please forgive my black-hearted soul!'

Although pain throbbed in her sacred horn, and in agony her innocent shoulder bled, the unicorn knew the need for pity and this is what she said: 'Warrior, save yourself while you can. This was your wish, so now, to save your lost soul, you must wish for something to heal my wound.'

The warrior had been unthinking in his deeds; he had craved power and done anything to satisfy the means. Now, with true remorse, he wished to heal her at any price and in the very instant of his wishing he lost his human form to become a small tree with dark green leaves that were trimmed in brightest gold. The unicorn ate several leaves then sure enough, the torn, blood-drenched hole closed over, as if it had never been!

Angered, the sorcerer cursed aloud. He must either run in fear or deal with the living unicorn. With sadness in her velvet eyes, the unicorn turned to him and spoke: 'You are an outcast. You are ugly, damaged, and very, very sad. You have my pity, so I too make a wish and this is what I say: 'Let the gold the warrior paid you, forever disappear. And may you be shunned by all until the day you make amends.'

The riches that the warrior had bestowed vanished, and were never seen again, and so it was that the sorcerer knew defeat, and he cursed with anguish and angry tears.

The unicorn had fulfilled her task. She knew there was nothing left to do, so with the speed of birds and the legs of horse, she galloped away, far away.

For a while, Wish was quiet again.

From wishes, from wishes
Come all your desires…
From desires
Come all your dreams

From dreams, from dreams
Come all your hopes…
From hopes
Come your schemes, and your plans

Be brave, be brave
Don't hide or hold back…
Endeavour
And you will aspire

Believe, believe
Trust in yourself…
Let your heart and your mind
Conspire

From wishes, from wishes
Come all your dreams…
And from dreams come
Your wisdom and power…

Candela's Gift

Walking through a forest alone, a female unicorn came upon an uncommon tree. It was a giant amongst trees. It was pure white, and a thick mist flowed from it. Beneath the tree, there lay a single fallen branch.

Curiously, the unicorn nudged the branch and, mysteriously, found herself transported inside the tree. In the very centre of the tree, there was a raised mound. On it there lay a thick parchment. The unicorn approached. As she did so, words etched on the parchment glowed: *The Book of Divination*.

As she walked closer, the parchment unravelled, as if beckoning her to read.

Upon learning everything that was written there, the unicorn understood that it was time to leave. As soon as she had the thought, she found herself outside once more. Thick white mist poured from the tree's limbs over and through her, until she glowed.

Picking the fallen branch off the ground with her teeth, the unicorn passed all the things she had learned from the parchment into it, so she could keep the knowledge always.

She named the branch *Staff of the Unimaginable*.

CHAPTER 1

Paths that criss and cross

The Bridge of the Long Forgotten. That's what it said on the sign. It was such a small sign that Rielle almost didn't see it, but as she paused with indecision, she looked down to a patch of burnished wood and read the warning words. She stopped. Pud trod carefully to the edge of the brink.

'Come away, Pud!' Rielle snapped. 'Isn't it bad enough that we've lost Far these past few days?'

The dog stepped back from the ledge, his paw dislodging a pile of stones. With heavy foreboding, Rielle and Pud lost sight of them, well before they landed in the heaving waters below. The wind changed direction and tickled the distant walls of the canyon with a moan.

Rielle shifted her slight frame restlessly from leg to leg. Squinting shrewdly from large brown eyes, she scanned the bridge carefully then sighed with annoyance.

'The Bridge of the Long Forgotten,' she murmured, as she hunkered down next to the dog. 'What do you think, boy?' she whispered, as if whispering could make them even better friends, or greater accomplices, than they already were. 'What do you think, my faithful Pud? Should we cross this rickety wreck, or should we see if Far will catch up with us first?'

Far, the butterfly, often wandered away, but she'd never been gone for so long before.

Suddenly, a whip of wind channelled like a bullet, up and around the canyon walls, buffeting Rielle and Pud and shaking the bridge, as a giant would with a toy. Pud nudged Rielle with his big black body and then placed a paw onto her shoe.

Rielle looked around. They stood on a bare, stricken patch of ground where nothing grew and the trail ended. Canyon walls stretched as far up and down as they could see. There was not even a shrub to shelter them on the deserted ledge. Rielle shuddered, remembering a fateful night when she and Pud had been lost and were forced to hide inside an ancient tree. Now, evening drew near. A pale slice of hunter's moon rose, gleaming in the first elegant coatings of dusk. Rielle knew what they had to do.

'It's now or never, Pud,' she grimaced. 'We have no choice but to cross that fury below. This is the only way to go.'

She stood. Fastening her travel-sack securely around her waist, she took her hat off and pushed it deeply inside. Rielle loved her hat. It was her favourite colour and long ago, a dear friend had given it to her. One fateful day, she had almost lost her hat on another cliff edge. She grinned awkwardly at the memory, tossed her long plait over her shoulder and glanced up. Pud was already at the foot of the bridge. Timidly, he placed a paw on the first shaky plank.

'Wait Pud, let me go first!' Rielle called, grim-faced. But it was too late.

With unusual disobedience, and with the zeal of a dog, Pud charged over the bridge and was almost across when another whip of wind roared through the canyon, sweeping him off his feet.

'Pud!' Rielle bawled.

An echo bounced her cry chillingly off the canyon walls. For a fateful second she watched in horror as Pud hovered, suspended in mid-air, scrambling at empty space with quick, desperate movements and surprise raging in his eyes. Then he began to fall.

Rielle was already running. Throwing herself upon the bridge's swaying framework, she leapt for her best friend. Pud yipped, despite himself, as his mistress seized him with a grunt, and heaved him frantically back to safety.

Rielle and Pud lay stunned and trembling as the wind pounded the ancient bridge. Below them, the torrent roared and frothed, wicked, white and jagged. If a river ever had jaws, then they were looking at it.

Shakily, Pud stood. With sharp barks, he urged Rielle to keep moving.

Rielle went to get up, but her travel-sack was caught. She tugged. It was stuck! She tried to get up and kneel, but the sack held fast. With a sickening lurch, she glimpsed the white water below. Stricken, she looked away.

Pud licked her face and whined.

The bridge swayed, and the wind began to squeal.

'Get off!' Rielle yelled at the dog. 'Run! I'll be with you as soon as I can!'

Pud glanced at the pathway beyond and then looked at his mistress. He lay down beside her.

'Hooley bondooley!' Rielle swore. 'Don't make me yell at you Pud! You know it makes me angry when I lose my temper! This bridge can't take the weight of us both!'

The dog didn't budge. Weight or no weight, he was not leaving her side now. The bridge creaked. Strands of rope stretched and tensed. Icy fear cringed along Rielle's spine. Jets of water from the torrent below reached up, like arms, towards her.

In a whisper, Rielle heard someone, or something, call her name.

Just then, the rope beneath her nose began to split and fray. Stunned, Rielle watched it unravel, until finally, it snapped. The wooden plank it held dropped lazily into the mouth of the yawning river.

Desperate, Rielle hauled on her travel-sack. With a rip, it came free, just as several other planks surrendered, and dripped like the icy sweat on her brow into the triumphant torrent. Immediately, Pud leapt the last steps of the bridge, clearing the way for her to run. Sickened, Rielle slipped and scrambled, then lurched clear of the bridge to join him.

That was all the bridge needed. It snapped like brittle toffee. With one last, lingering sigh, it slid almost gracefully into the raging water below, leaving a yawning gap between the cliffs.

Rielle gaped, white-faced, as they watched it fall.

'Even if we wanted to,' she rasped, 'there's no going back now!'

'Well done,' chirped a voice.

Pud barked, sneezed with joy then jumped up and down.

Looking up, Rielle grinned then laughed. 'Far! You're back!'

'Let's get off this ledge!' squealed the butterfly, as a frenzied roar of wind pelted up the canyon with unreasonable fury.

Throwing herself more than running, Rielle followed Pud's lead and hid in the hollow of a rock face. She glanced back. Thunderstruck, she watched the wind surround Far. With a shriek of triumph, it whisked the bright blue butterfly to the entrance of the channel, and out of sight.

'Far!' Rielle roared. *Surely, it was some mistake?* She turned helplessly to Pud, but he stared miserably into the distance, his large tan eyebrows furrowed.

'She'll be fine, Pud,' Rielle wheezed, 'surely, surely. After all, she is Hope's butterfly.'

They sat in wounded silence, as the wind scratched the cliff face, like a wolf hungry for a meal. Doggedly, Rielle finally scrambled to her feet.

'Come on, Pud,' she growled, 'I need to think.' With menace on her face, she began to climb the ragged canyon path.

There it was again. Someone, or something, whispering her name! Hesitantly, she stopped and looked back at the crevasse. Pud gazed up at his mistress with clever amber eyes. Rielle looked down at him and gritted her teeth.

'There's nothing for it, Pud,' she breathed, as she rested a hand on his head. 'We, well, we have to go back to Wish!'

Pud yipped. Rielle shuddered and caught her breath. 'We've lost Far. I think she's gone, really gone, and, well, she's not mine to lose.' Rielle's eyes misted. 'We have to tell Hope. It's the right thing to do.'

Frowning, she drew her cloak about her as if it could protect her from unseen things. 'I thought Far would be with us through to the end; that is, at least until I found my dream.'

Rielle... someone whispered her name.

'Did you hear that, Pud?' Rielle glanced around. 'Did you hear someone say my name?'

Pud had no chance to answer as the wind screeched around them. Small rocks tinkled menacingly from the cliffs above as a rumble shook the canyon walls. With grim understanding, Rielle and Pud looked up. A huge boulder was tumbling like a fat marshmallow towards them.

'Run!' Rielle bellowed, but Pud was already on the move.

The Bridge of the Long Forgotten... Rielle's thoughts galloped as her legs tried to keep up... *and this must be the path of the long forgotten, judging by the mess it's in!*

She braced herself and struggled over the jutting, broken trail with its cracks, weeds and rocky out-thrusts. Pud raced sure-footed, looking back to check on her.

The path narrowed as they ran, leaving them just a few short feet from the drop. Rielle picked up the pace. If the boulder hit the track as they ran on this narrow ledge, it would throw them like bouncing balls over the edge!

She stumbled briefly, righted herself, and once more looked up. With renewed panic, she sprinted after her fleeing dog. Above them, the boulder boomed a warning.

Like a godsend, the path suddenly widened and spread into a large opening that ran inside the mountain. Rielle and Pud hurtled into the dark, vacant gap as if it were an offering of a life raft from a sinking ship, rather than an unknown threshold that beckoned beyond their reason. Gasping for breath, they stopped inside the cave entrance, relief flooding them like a rush of spring warmth. Outside, the boulder landed. The mountain heaved, convulsing.

Helplessly, Rielle and Pud lost their footing. Like wretched rag dolls, powerless and deafened, they rolled down inside the mountain, deep into its murky grey depths. Pud yipped a bleak question to his mistress. Winded, Rielle found she had no voice.

Finally, after minutes that felt like hours, the booming and shaking stopped. Slamming to a halt in a pile of dirt, Pud found his legs, tripped, righted himself, snorted, sat down and looked around.

'Hooley bondooley,' Rielle wheezed through clenched teeth, 'one day I'll swap all this excitement for a boring life!' She groaned and lay still, with her eyes tightly closed. 'Things weren't meant to go like this. We were on the right path, according to Far, but now everything's gone wrong!'

Pud howled. Rielle's skin crawled. Pud howled plaintively again. Reluctantly, Rielle opened her eyes. Hesitantly, she sat up. She winced; she was covered in bruises. Dust billowed around them, but a faint light grew brighter as the dust slowly settled. Pud grunted.

'Dragon's claws!' Rielle gasped. 'Pud, the walls glitter like gold! What do you think it means?'

Even as Rielle said the words, a small tower of dust swelled in their direction and then stopped. A creature stood before them.

Rielle was accustomed to meeting strangers and odd newcomers that resembled no one she had ever seen before, but it still made her uncomfortable. She touched the star-scar on her brow, but she didn't have a headache, so it wasn't warning her of danger.

The star-scar that the mighty unicorns had etched carefully on her brow; between it and faithful Pud, she always felt protected.

Rielle sneezed then frowned. Where were they?

The creature was staring. It looked odd, but not sinister.

'Hello,' Rielle whispered. She had learned that no one was prepared to be nice to you if you weren't at least polite to them.

'*Rotisiv U,*' the creature answered.

'Um,' Rielle sighed, 'do you speak human?'

'*Hewwmaan,*' it replied.

'Yes, that's it,' Rielle encouraged, 'you know, do you speak the way I do?' She poked herself on the chest with a finger.

The creature peered down at her. Guardedly, Rielle stood up. The creature was only as high as her chin. It gazed up at her with one eye. Its other eye was covered by a large black eye-patch. In a sudden movement, it pushed Rielle's arm with its thumb. Rielle gaped. The creature had a small suction cup built into its thumb! Briefly, the suction seemed to burn her arm, but her star-scar still showed her there was no harm here. The creature grinned, released the thumb sucker, giggled from its half-moon mouth, scratched a spot where there was a missing ear and slowly wiggled its tail.

'Hewman!' it repeated, then scratched the bald patch on its head.

Pud sneezed, a happy sneeze, then barked at the little semi-humanoid, who wore a brown tunic and brown sandals on its three-toed feet. The creature looked at Pud, and then it also sneezed, barked and sneezed again. Pud lay down with his belly upmost as the creature bent over and scratched him on his favourite spot, right near his chest. Pud wagged his tail and the creature wagged *its* tail. Rielle watched on, perplexed.

'Who are you?' she gasped.

The creature blinked its uncovered eye and then, as if to confuse Rielle completely, it moved the eye-patch over, settled it neatly on the other eye and blinked up at her again.

Rielle frowned. Both of the creature's eyes seemed perfectly fine, so why did it need the eye-patch? She sighed. Nothing was as she expected. Life had become very unusual since meeting the unicorn herd!

The creature coughed, cleared its throat, looked sweetly at Rielle and then poked itself in the chest with its thumb as it wiggled the rest of its fingers.

'I,' it began, smiling happily, 'I am *Eerht ytnewt On*,

21

Number Twenty Three of the First Ones.'

'Oh? Uh... the First Ones?' Rielle queried.

Pud sat down and scratched. The dust was itchy and he loved meeting strangers.

The creature blinked solemnly. 'The First Ones,' he repeated.

Rielle was puzzled. 'I'm Rielle, and this is Pud. Um, how should I say your name, exactly?'

'Eerht ytnewt *On!*'

Rielle did her best to pronounce the name but after several attempts, it still didn't sound right.

'Are the First Ones old?' she asked, as a distraction.

'Ahhhh... old? Yes, the oldest. The First Ones!' Eerht ytnewt On retorted, shrugging his shoulders, as if it were obvious.

Rielle paused, annoyed with herself, and then thought of something she hoped might work. 'Would it be alright then, not meaning any disrespect, if I just called you *Old*, then? I mean, only until I work it out?'

Eerht ytnewt On pulled his eye-patch up onto his forehead. He peered sincerely at Rielle from wide eyes. Then, as if to make sure she wasn't teasing, he tapped one of his three-toed feet in a gentle rhythm and placed his fingertips together.

'Old,' he muttered, shutting his eyes, 'Old... Old... Old. Old is interesting,' Eerht ytnewt On declared. 'Old is accepted.' He peeked at Rielle, winked at Pud, promptly pulled his eye-patch down over one eye, then sat on the ground and crossed his feet.

Pud wagged his tail and grinned.

Rielle…

Rielle jumped. 'Did you hear that?' she cried. 'It's that voice again, calling me, whispering my name!'

'Sit, Rielle,' Old urged sincerely, 'sit, be still, be quiet and listen. Old has words to share with you.'

'But, but, did you hear it?' Rielle asked, as she reluctantly sat. 'That voice - it's been calling me for days!'

Pud whined then sat up with his ears pricked.

'What is it, Pud?' Rielle squinted into the dark.

Slowly, Pud walked toward a long narrow passage at the end of the cave that was visible now that the dust had settled. He sniffed the air and then the ground. Rielle went to get up.

'Stay, Rielle,' Old entreated, 'stay and sit, sit and stay.'

Rielle looked hard at the odd creature. His uncovered eye was unexpectedly serious and so was his half-moon mouth.

Pud suddenly lost interest in his sniffing and came back to sit with them. He kept his eyes on the narrow passage, his ears still pricked in silent vigil.

Old said nothing, and the cavern became as still as a graveyard and just as cold. Rielle shivered. All around them, the walls glittered and shone. She had to say something.

'Is that real gold?' she whispered into the silence. 'It looks like it is.'

Old glanced at the walls. 'What is *real* gold?' he sighed. 'Gold is gold, my walls are gold.' His mouth turned downward in an unhappy arc. 'My walls are gold,' he repeated. 'I sit in gold but the others are lost; me, Number Twenty Three of the First Ones, alone with gold, but not with the others.'

He looked up at Rielle and placed his suction thumb onto Pud.

Pud licked Old's hand and placed a paw onto one of his feet.

Rielle was amazed. Pud did that to her! It was their special bond. She looked closely at Old. There was something here that she wasn't sure about. Oddly, Pud thought Old was wonderful.

'Who, uh… who are the others?' she asked hesitantly.

Old grunted. 'Old has words to share, but not here.' He looked around. 'Here the mountain rocks and rolls.' He nodded toward the narrow passage. 'Home is safest. Follow Old.'

In a single leap, Old sprung to his feet and bowed politely to Rielle.

Pud barked and was already on his way.

'Wait Pud,' Rielle scolded, 'you've already gone off half-baked once today! This time you can wait for me.'

She turned to Old. 'I can't stay long, you understand. I'm on a mission.' She wrinkled her nose. 'Two missions, now.'

Old sniffed the air and squinted kindly at her. 'You are sad,' he whispered, 'you are sad. Old has tea for sadness. Come, visit. Missions are best after tea!'

He bowed again to Rielle and then, gently, he took her left hand in his right one and urged her to follow.

Surprised, Rielle noticed that his hand was softer than doe hair and twice as smooth. She looked forward to joining him for tea. His touch was the very core of kindness and her heart warmed to him, despite his oddness and black eye-patch.

As if to confirm his words, the mountain outside shuddered as another huge boulder plunged to its end. The floor shook, dust rose and then all was quiet.

Old still held Rielle's hand. 'Come for tea,' he invited matter-of-factly again, as he led her toward the narrow passage in the wall.

CHAPTER 2

Free to be

Far felt the wind stretch and twist her fragile body, turning her into a flurry of wings then rolling her like a bent banana. She struggled valiantly to straighten herself and to gain the right to fly, but the wind gripped her in its iron fist, roaring with monotonous victory around the canyon. Far suspected it would never end.

Just as exhaustion began to strip the butterfly of her natural confidence, the wind punched a hole into the mighty river and plunged her down into its depths. Sucked into the forceful mainstream, Far struggled for futile moments, then stopped fighting a power mightier than herself. In a churning, frantic mass, the white water pulled her under, deeper, deeper, until all daylight disappeared and she lay inactive and limp.

The next thing Far knew, whiskers were tickling her. She opened her eyes. She was on dry land! She tried to move, but she was waterlogged. The whiskers tickled her again before two black eyes looked deeply into her own. As if satisfied, the eyes moved away, and shortly after, music began to play.

Far gasped, drawing deep breaths into her lungs.

'That was close,' she groaned. 'I don't want a bath, ever again!' In a soggy half-movement, she sat up just in time to see the tail and two goat-like feet of the piping faun who had rescued her, move away into the trees. His music followed.

'Thank you!' Far called.

Briefly, he turned his small dancing body to wave, and then he was gone.

'Saved,' Far grumbled, relieved. 'Saved by the music-playing faun.' She frowned. 'This place is familiar. Where am I?'

Groggily, she tried to untangle her soggy and bent bits, but the bush she sat on swayed back and forth, despite the fact that there was no wind. As she struggled to find her balance, understanding struck her.

'Oh no,' Far cried, 'I'm in Wish! This can't be good. I'm supposed to be with Rielle in the outside world, not here in Wish!'

She tried to leap upward and fly away, but one of her wings clung, with sticky determination, to the leaf she sat upon. She tugged, but it wouldn't budge. She twisted and turned, but her wing lay trapped. The bush swayed so hard that Far thought it would pull the wing from her body, and that would be a disaster!

'Sad little bush, aren't you,' Far observed kindly, despite her quandary. 'You only have one leaf.'

With another mighty heave, the bush whirled around. In desperation for her wing, Far grabbed the leaf and held on tightly. As if enough had not gone wrong, the little leaf tore right off the bush. Far was sent hurtling through the air to land upside down in a clod of soft earth.

'Ooooowch!' she bellowed. 'Enough is enough!' With a final enormous tug, she freed her wing, righted herself, then stood and shook, sending the last drops of water flying, leaving her to be herself again.

'Thank you,' croaked a voice behind her.

Surprised, Far leapt upwards, ready to flee.

'Don't go,' called the voice, 'you saved me! I'm free! I'm finally free!'

Curiosity forced Far to look, as she swung backwards, fluttering warily out of reach. A young man stood looking up at her, his face etched in a broad grin. He was handsome - even Far could tell that much - although humans were not her speciality. His clothes were dusty, though, and very tattered and torn. He bent over, picked up a broad-brimmed hat that was trimmed with a feather, and then beamed up at her.

'You… wee blue butterfly,' he laughed, poking the air with a finger, 'have saved my sorry skin!'

Far flinched beyond his reach. 'How so?' Far had no idea what he was talking about. She waited with hooded eyes and a half-hearted frown.

'You tore off the last leaf,' the young man explained jubilantly.

'You mean that's a good thing?' Far was confused. She looked over his shoulder. The bush was no longer there!

'Where's the bush gone?' she asked.

The young man clapped his chest with one hand, smacked his leg with the other, did an awkward dance and hooted. Frightened birds fled from a nearby tree.

'Here,' he called, 'here! It was *me*, but it's not me *any more!* I'm free, don't you see, and *you* did it!' He pressed his face as close to Far as she would let him.

'Hmm, no,' Far grumbled, 'I really don't see. You'll have to explain, and hurry up. I've got things to do!'

But the young man wasn't interested in Far's problems.

'So,' he said, talking over her, 'how do I get out of this place?'

Far decided she did not like him. Despite his good looks and charming smile, Far found him bothersome. It was obvious that once he had been the bush and now he was the young, human male standing in front of her, but all seemed well, and Far had her own problems to solve. She wasn't really surprised by the turn of events; after all, this *was* Wish and anything was possible! She looked him up and down again, then turned and flew away.

'Wait! Don't go!' he called. 'Didn't you hear me? How do I get out of this place?'

Far picked up speed. 'The same way you got here!' she bellowed as she flew. Running footsteps followed her, and with practised ease, Far flew higher and faster.

'You've got to help me,' puffed the young man. 'I've been here so long I can't remember what to do... you know, how to leave this place and go... well, go home.'

'I'm busy,' Far rejoined. 'I have trouble. I've lost my human and I have to find Hope.'

'Hope?' the young man puffed. 'You mean Hope's someone you know? Like a person or something?'

Far felt his snigger, rather than heard it. 'You're annoying me,' she called, hovering several feet above his flamboyant hat, 'and you obviously have no idea about things and definitely no respect. Hope is my boss, and unlike you, he listens when others talk!'

The young man looked helplessly at her. 'Please,' he pleaded, 'please help me. I'm completely lost.'

Far knew that if she hadn't been so preoccupied, she would have been more her cheerful chatty self, and not the slightest bit impolite. She hesitated, and then let down her guard. The young man seemed genuine. Despite her urgency, she hovered level with his eyes. She looked coolly at him.

'What's your name?' she asked.

The young man smiled wanly. 'Uh, Will. You can call me Will.'

'Okay,' Far replied, keeping a distance, 'I might help you.'

Will smiled charmingly.

'But first,' Far bargained, 'I want to know why you were a bush.'

The light left Will's eyes. 'Oh, that,' he fidgeted.

'You have to be honest with me,' Far fired at him. 'I'm in no mood for games. I told you, I have things to do!'

'Why do you want to know?' he almost pouted.

'Because,' Far snapped, 'we *are* in Wish and you *are* human.'

Will frowned. 'What has that go to do with you?' he asked stubbornly. 'All I asked for is help to get out of here.'

'Ah, and so you did,' Far quipped, 'but if I know humans they don't spend their time as a small tree, unless something very unusual has happened, even in Wish!'

Will remained silent.

'Wish comes from the minds of humans after all,' Far bellowed at his lack of response, 'so what happens to humans here is their own doing!'

Will glanced around uncertainly. 'Why do you say that?' he muttered.

'Because,' Far snapped, losing patience with the cut and thrust, 'because, although humans are not my speciality, that being more Hope's department, by what I know, they tend to often be, well… rather attached to themselves, if you know what I mean? Most humans wouldn't waste time sitting around as a bush!'

The young man began to interrupt, but Far cut him short.

'Hurry up,' she roared, 'I have urgent things to do. Either tell me or don't, but unless you tell me very soon, you can get help from someone else!'

Will paused. Trees swayed calmly and birds chirped freely, and he wanted to go home. It looked like the butterfly was his only chance. He put his hands in his pockets and avoided her eyes.

'I, uh… *tridshooanicrn*,' he mumbled.

'I'm sorry,' Far fluttered closer, 'I didn't catch that. Would you speak up?'

Looking at the ground, Will repeated himself.

'I still can't hear you!' Far cried, and threatened, with a flapping movement, to fly away.

'Alright!' Will called. 'Don't go!' He looked Far in the eyes, took a deep breath, swallowed, and pulled his hands from his pockets. His blue eyes flinched from a private thought, but then clearly, and with utmost precision, he stated, 'I tried to shoot a unicorn.'

Far was prepared for anything but that. 'You did what?' she gasped. 'And... and you expect me to help you? Don't you know when someone shoots at a unicorn that it's a big mistake?'

Torment jumbled in Will's eyes.

But it was enough for Far. 'You are a villain!' she hollered, and promptly forgot about helping him. With speed that even she didn't think she had, Far thrust upward and flew for all her worth.

'No, no, I promise you, I promise you, I'm not!' Will hurtled after her.

Far, however, ducked and dived amongst tall sighing trees and disappeared from sight.

Will stopped running. Bewildered, he looked around. He was alone and lost, in the solitary silence of Wish.

CHAPTER 3

How unicorns know things

A slice of sun tested the morning, decided that it liked the day and continued to climb the glowing sky. Into a small beam of light, a white shape left a clump of trees and paused. Then, urgently, it careered around and disappeared from sight.

Benny, the unicorn, thundered through thick forest undergrowth, leaping rocks and fallen trees, his hooves striking tiny sparks, to send messages through the dawn. Galloping down gullies as if the very furies were after his neck, his mane and tail streamed behind him like flags flying in the wind.

...

At home in the forest, the unicorn herd was nervous. They knew that Benny, the little unicorn, was fleeing for his life.

Trilling urgent messages into the speckled air, Benny's father, Coraggio, pawed the ground then listened.

'Run,' he urged the herd, 'run and do not stop until we find Benny.'

In a wave of glittering white light, the unicorns grouped together and clattered with unusual noise and haste to find the missing one.

...

Benny stopped in a narrow gully. Small daybreak noises scratched the air and caught the edges of his breathing. Through the sensitive fibres of his horn, he sensed the herd searching for him. His white coat glistened from the effort of his galloping but he knew he could not rest for long. The pain in his head was fading; he was ahead of his enemy, but that was not enough.

Leaping from the gully, he hurtled down the side of a hill. With renewed strength, he galloped at breakneck speed, until at last he saw what he was searching for. The ocean lay ahead. He plunged into its foamy surf and disappeared from sight. The air stood still, and all was quiet, as the shores of Wish lapped peacefully.

Time passed. Then, from a grove of trees, a figure emerged. The figure walked the charming shoreline. It too seemed tempted to take the plunge. Instead, it shook a fist at the warm wafting air, turned tail and slunk away. Where the figure walked there remained slimy pits of stench-filled rancid mud.

...

Rising from the ocean, Benny landed on the shores of a pond, far from Wish. Stillness greeted him. It was night in the forest and the moon lingered lightly above. Benny's horn no longer hurt. He was safe!

'They're looking for you again,' whistled a voice.

'Oobaat!' Benny gasped. 'I have terrible news!'

Hooves thundered on the stone-cluttered path with a deafening assault, as the unicorn herd rounded a bend. They stopped, as one, on the banks of the wishing pond.

'Benny,' his mother, Candela, exclaimed, 'what possessed you to venture forth alone?'

Benny looked imploringly at his parents and the herd. 'I have terrible news!' he cried.

'Let that wait,' Coraggio urged, 'we must attend to the Ritual of Return.'

Not even Benny was willing to argue about that. If not for the Ritual of Return, he might never have made it back to the forest from Wish, at this or any other time. Quickly the unicorns came forward, one by one. They each tapped Benny on the forehead gently, leaving trails of white light to flow and trickle down his horn, renewing his union with the herd.

Oobaat, the gatekeeper, watched on. He was used to rumours of the goings on in Wish. After all, hadn't he been guarding the wishing pond for almost longer than even he could remember? He wondered patiently what the young unicorn would tell. Rana, the frog, Oobaat's helper, sensed the seriousness in Benny's voice and for once he, too, sat and quietly looked on.

The ritual ended. The unicorns stood still. White light surrounded them in a misty glow.

'This time,' Coraggio muttered in a deep, low voice, 'this time we were all prepared to take the plunge, if that is what it took to find you young Benny.'

Benny gasped. 'All of you would have gone to Wish?

The entire herd? After what we know?'

Candela flinched even as she answered. 'Yes dear, this time we thought we'd lost you and we would have taken the chance.'

Benny hung his head and gave this last news careful thought. He looked up then, as the herd waited. 'I'm sorry, but I had to go.' He caught his breath. 'I had a feeling that something was wrong.'

Coraggio nudged his cherished child. 'Next time, let us know,' he chided, 'and don't go there alone.'

Benny shrugged. 'It all happened so suddenly that I couldn't wait.'

'Tell us then,' implored Candela, 'tell us what you've learned.'

Benny snorted. 'I had to find Rielle and Pud.'

The herd nodded. Now they understood. Benny had taken the task of watching over the human girl and so, of course, she and Benny shared a special bond.

Oobaat heaved his tortoise body from the pond. 'Wait if you would,' he interrupted, settling himself in front of the herd. 'Let me get comfortable before you begin.'

The forest rustled in the deep of night.

'I have terrible news,' Benny repeated, his eyes filled with alarm. 'I sensed that things were not right for Rielle. I wondered if, by some misfortune, she had returned to Wish, but I didn't find her there.' He tossed his head before going on. 'I learned something, though. It's about the Sorcerer of Great Contempt!'

The herd recoiled but waited.

Benny breathed the next words like the disappointment they were.

'He has an accomplice in the outside world.'

The herd gasped.

'How can that be?' breathed Candela. 'How can it be that this has happened? He should be harmlessly exiled in Wish.' She looked at Coraggio, but he was willing Benny on.

Benny nodded. 'For now the sorcerer can only make the wind do his work, but who knows when he might do more… or worse?'

'The wind now does his work?' Coraggio challenged. 'How do you know? We have no evidence of this in the forest.'

Benny shook his head. 'He can't reach the forest, but in other parts of the outside world he can command the wind. I've seen it!'

'So it isn't too powerful yet… this new power of his?' Oobaat pressed fervently.

'No, not so powerful yet,' Benny agreed. 'Not yet!'

'How do you know this?' Oobaat prompted nervously.

Benny pawed a patch of ground and tossed his mane. 'I was walking through the river-lands, thinking of Rielle and Pud. Suddenly, the river began to churn where it usually travels slowly. I thought it was strange. Even as I had the thought, a ball of wind shot up from the river and into the air. Before I had a chance to wonder, the ball of wind was gone. I've never seen anything like it.'

Benny's eyes flickered over the transfixed herd. 'Then the ball of wind returned. With a screech, it plunged back into the river.' He paused and caught his breath.

'In that moment I felt a tug on my heart. I knew Rielle

and Pud needed me. I asked the river where the ball of wind had come from and the river told me it came from *Wish*. I had to know what was happening so I galloped to the wishing pond, told Oobaat I was going to Wish, and then... I went.'

'Ah, so that was your hurry,' Oobaat sighed.

Coraggio frowned at the gatekeeper.

Oobaat shrugged. 'You know the rules,' he stated. 'I can't stop anyone, or change what they do. I just record their passing and let them through.'

'It's not his fault,' Benny cut in, 'it was urgent. Oobaat tried to ask me to wait, but I just had to go!'

The herd nodded.

'So, what did you find in Wish?' Candela urged.

Benny looked defiantly at the herd. 'I couldn't sense Rielle there, so... so I tracked the sorcerer down.'

The herd shook their heads and trilled loudly.

'Benny,' Coraggio glared, 'that was too dangerous!'

Benny hung his head, but only for a second. 'At first the sorcerer didn't see me,' he gasped, 'and that's when I saw him do it. I saw him make another ball of wind and then I heard him make a spell. He sent the wind-ball off to do some mischief, but when he finished, he sensed my presence.' Benny rolled his eyes. 'I had to run then, like I've never run before!'

Candela whickered. 'Thank goodness you arrived home safely. It might have ended horribly.'

The herd shifted nervously.

'Hmm,' Coraggio murmured, 'this news calls for drastic measures.' With a deliberate glance, he fixed his gaze on Oobaat.

The gatekeeper stood. Averting his eyes from Coraggio's penetrating stare, he edged toward the pond.

'Oh no,' Oobaat crooned, shaking his head, 'no, no and no.'

'I said *drastic measures*,' Coraggio called to Oobaat's retreating back. 'Oobaat, surely you knew this day might come? We all did.' Coraggio nodded at the herd, and they nodded back. 'And now it seems the worst might be here!'

'I guard the wishing pond, remember?' Oobaat replied. 'So, I can't leave my important job, now can I?'

Coraggio wasn't giving up. He cantered in front of the tortoise just before Oobaat plunged into the pond.

'Hear me, Oobaat,' he breathed. 'You are one of a few that still remain! We need you. The forest needs you. Perhaps the whole outside world needs you!'

Coraggio stomped a commanding hoof. 'Whilst the sorcerer's power was trapped in Wish, things were bad enough, but Wish is, well, *Wish*, and we can't interfere there. But if not you, then who can help us now?'

'I can do the pond thingy!' Rana cut in, surprising them all. The frog's goggle eyes darted to meet Coraggio's. 'Tell him, tell him, I'm more experienced now, and I can do the pond thingy! You know, ask everyone why they're going to Wish, record their names and time of passing through. I've memorised all the rules.'

'Pond thingy?' Oobaat groaned. 'The most important duties and greatest responsibilities, he calls *thingies!*'

Oobaat turned to Coraggio. 'Now, can you see why

I can't leave my job?' Then, promptly, before Coraggio could argue further, Oobaat dove into the pond and disappeared from sight.

The herd moaned, crestfallen.

Coraggio and Candela's eyes met. Coraggio nodded at the herd. Unspoken, the message was understood.

Standing on the banks of the pond, Coraggio peered in.

'Oobaat,' he compelled,' if you won't help us willingly, I will be forced to call upon the *Oath of Spirit, Fire, Air, Earth and Water!*'

The herd winced and held their breaths. This was a challenge! They recalled the last time the oath was summoned.

Moments passed. Only bubbles came to the pond's surface.

At last, Coraggio turned to the herd. 'It looks like I misjudged the tortoise. I thought he had a greater sense of justice.' He shook his head. 'But no, it appears he's become lazy and tiresome.'

'What will we do?' asked Benny.

Coraggio hesitated. Moonlight glinted shyly through the trees.

'Well,' Coraggio finally whispered, 'it seems I have no choice. Gather around. We must raise the Oath!'

CHAPTER 4

Hooley dooley and bondooley

Clasping Rielle's hand securely in his own, Old led the way deeper inside the mountain. Dripping water tinkled faintly into barely visible, motionless pools. Long stalactites, designed by time, formed unlikely shapes, trickling like honey from the ceiling of the cavern.

Rielle looked around. 'Do you like living here?' she whispered, doubtfully.

Old pondered before he answered. 'Once,' he began solemnly, 'I would climb this mountain, just gently climbing for her beauty and joy.' He paused and sighed. 'I watched the river, I smelled the flowers, and I knew the sunset and sunrise. I waited for those happy moments when the rain builds its bow. Then I built the Bridge of the Long Forgotten, and after that I built the path, in case a friend should come by... you understand?' He smiled fleetingly. 'I built a sturdy wall I called the Serpent's Way, and then I found I could not stop, I had to be doing all the time.' He blinked up at Rielle. 'But I forgot to build myself a home.'

They stepped under and around an enormous stalactite that glowed in the golden light. The mountain's silence grew deeper.

Old sighed. 'I became so very, very tired, but still I carried on. I worked from morning through the night and into long, long years.' He grunted. 'Then one day, I walked inside the mountain, and since, I have never seen the day.' They were almost at the passage entrance. 'Do I like to live here, you ask?' he whispered.

'Well, do you?' Rielle urged softly.

Old squeezed her hand. 'I miss the sun, I miss the rain. I miss the beauty of the mountain and the river and the wind.'

'Then why do you stay?' Rielle asked kindly.

Old waited before answering. The only sounds were their breathing and soft footfalls.

'I forget how to leave,' was all Old replied.

Rielle looked down at the First One and in the glow from the golden walls she saw the sadness in his eye.

'I made the walls of gold,' he whispered, 'in memory of the others, but it doesn't bring them back; it doesn't bring them back. I live buried in the mountain when once I climbed its walls. The sun once warmed my body, the wind would whisper tales. I was willing to take chances, but now I'm underground.'

They had arrived at the doorway to the passage. The entrance loomed. Rielle held Pud close.

Old turned and bowed to Rielle. 'Welcome to my den,' he offered courteously.

Pud sniffed the air. There was something unusual but interesting about Old's strange lair. With timid steps Pud went first, followed by Rielle and then the First One.

'Oh,' Rielle gasped, 'there's more gold in here than out there!'

They were in a round chamber that glowed. Not only were the walls made of gold, but so was everything else: the small round table with its matching round chairs, the round cupboards, and the round fireplace.

'Sit,' Old urged, 'sit. I will make tea for sadness.'

Rielle and Pud sat down and watched Number Twenty Three of the First Ones perform the humble task of making tea. Everything he used was made of gold: the cups, saucers and spoons. From a gold jar he took out a lump of fresh crumbly cake. Slicing cake invitingly, he placed it on the table. Kindly, as an afterthought, Old took a roll of bread from the jar and placed it on the floor, on a bowl of gold, for Pud.

Rielle realised how hungry she was. 'If you don't go outside,' she couldn't help asking, 'how do you find your food?'

With finicky care Old brought a gigantic steaming teapot to the table. He placed it down, sat on a chair and poured delicious smelling tea into a cup for Rielle. 'Would Pud like tea?' he asked.

Pud licked his lips. The roll of bread had been delicious! He wouldn't say no to tea.

'He's never had tea,' Rielle laughed, but Pud nudged Old under the table and the First One bent down to pour him some.

'Be careful Pud,' Rielle scolded, 'it's very, very hot!'

With large sad eyes Pud drooled and waited. *Tea was no fun if you had to wait.*

Old placed cake on a plate for Rielle. She thanked him and took a bite.

'This is delicious!' Rielle looked up, puzzled. 'How is

it you find your tasty food?'

The First One quickly gobbled an enormous slice of cake then smacked his lips. 'Old has words to share with you,' was all he replied before he began eating another enormous slice of cake.

Pud slurped his cooling tea then lay at Rielle's feet with his belly in the air.

'I don't want to be impolite,' Rielle stated before Old could begin to share his words, 'so I hope you'll understand that I can't stay very long. I'm very grateful for the tea and cake, but something happened today.'

She glanced at the First One. He seemed to be listening with half-closed eyes and a polite smile.

'You see, we, Pud and I, were on a mission, but now I have to change my plans. I have to go to the land of Wish,' Rielle continued regretfully. 'I have to find Hope and give him some bad news.'

Old jumped up with a start. The heavy gold chair he'd been sitting on fell to the floor, and the piece of cake he'd been eating flew halfway across the room.

Pud leapt away, his hackles rising, as dishes rattled and crashed to the floor. *What in blazes was going on?*

'Did you say Hope?' Old boomed.

Frightened, Rielle retreated toward the back wall of Old's den. Pud dashed to her side. His mistress might need him if they had to run.

Old stood frozen. His hands were splayed on the table and his uncovered eye bulged with some strange emotion.

'Did you say Hope?' he asked again with more control. 'Did you say *Hope*?'

Rielle was confused. Old had been so sweet and calm. 'Yes,' she whispered white-faced. 'Yes, I said, Hope.'

Old galloped around the table and looked urgently up at her.

'Eno tsrif a si epoh wonk uoy tnod?' he chirped. 'Tell me, does this Hope wear a brown cloak and brown sandals? Just like mine?'

'I... I don't know,' Rielle responded. 'I've never met Hope. Benny, the unicorn, found him for me.'

'A *Lilifel* found him for you?' Old boomed again.

Pud ducked his head and covered his ears with his paws. Old's behaviour was becoming outrageous.

'You have seen a Lilifel of late?' Old waited open-mouthed as he gaped at Rielle.

'What's a Lilifel?' she asked.

Old grabbed Rielle's hands and began to dance with her around his golden den.

'Lilifel, un-i-co-rn... same thing!' he exclaimed. 'So happy,' he cried, 'so happy! Dance with Old!'

Pud barked, sneezed, and jumped up and down. This was strange but it seemed to be safe.

'Old will share words another time,' Old bellowed. 'Now we go to find Hope, *Enin On*, Number Nine of the First Ones!'

With an iron grip he reeled Rielle around to a stop. Just as suddenly, and as strangely, he picked up the fallen chair and sat down.

'Sit,' he said. 'Before we leave, we must finish tea for sadness.'

CHAPTER 5

Softly softly catchee flutterby

Far knew she must quickly reach the Tower of Dreams.
With her mind racing, she checked over her shoulder.
The young man had become a speck in the distance. She
promptly forgot about him. Her concerns were much
bigger than he was, and her wing was sore.

Weakened by her ordeal, she settled on a tree to
see where she was. No wiser, she flew to the highest
branch. With a sigh of relief, she found what she was
looking for. In the distance, purple mountains reared
impressively from the Valley of Possibility. Nestled in
that valley was the Tower of Dreams, and Hope! Far's
plight was urgent, but her aching wing needed rest. She
decided to take a nap.

On the horizon, a flash of colour sped through the sky.
It dipped and rolled, then whooshed upward again. In a
kaleidoscope of green mother-of-pearl, its wings coursed
with tremendous power, yet looked like delicate jewels.
A rainbow dragon was playing. In a mystery of pure joy,
it rolled and jack-knifed, plummeted and dove, as if the
sky were an ocean in which it swam.

As it flew over the tree where Far slept, the dragon sneezed. Blue flames shot from its nose and the teeniest ember struck Far. She yowled, shocked from her snooze. Zooming past, the rainbow dragon heard her cry. Breathtakingly fast, it turned to investigate. With luck, this might be a meal!

Far was not accustomed to being grouchy. When she'd lived in the Tower of Dreams with Hope, there hadn't been anything to be grumpy about. Then, when she'd taken to travelling with Rielle, life had become so exciting that she barely needed to eat or sleep.

She stood and tested her wing. It still hurt. She was confused. How to fly all the way to the tower with a wing that needed time to rest? If the task hadn't been so important she would have bunked in the tree for as long as she needed, but reaching Hope was urgent. Only he would know how to get her back to Rielle.

Rielle was searching for her dream and Far was supposed to be helping her. That had been the pact.

Dismayed, Far hung her head. 'I have to think, think, think!'

Just then, Far's world went red. A huge scorching furnace held her trapped. She squealed. With a violent twist, she fluttered uselessly for terrifying moments, but almost immediately, the furnace went out. She slumped, relieved, and looked up timidly. A large yellow eye blinked eerily down at her.

Far looked into the eye. 'Flightlord!' she roared, and promptly, in a show of great affection, she bit the largest wart on the dragon's face as hard as she could. 'How glad am I to see you!'

The rainbow dragon chuckled. He raised an eyebrow.

'I saw Hope some days ago,' he quizzed, 'and he mentioned you were not in Wish. Are you being a naughty butterfly?'

'Oh Flightlord,' Far almost sobbed, 'let me tell you how I need your help now!'

'Hush, Far, don't you cry,' Flightlord crooned softly. 'Here, come sit on my nose and tell me what makes you sad.'

Little Far, Hope's butterfly, was born under a lucky star. That is why she was lent to Rielle, so Rielle could keep her own spirits high. As Far squeaked and squealed and told Flightlord her tale, the dragon began to soar, and so, as luck would have it, Far didn't strain her wing, because Flightlord flew her to the Tower of Dreams.

...

'*Blast! Begads! Boogers! Badzits! Begonias! Bagodachi! Bigbods! Blaaaaast!*'

Beneath the tree Far had been napping in, a very angry figure emerged. In a fit of usual temper, the Sorcerer of Great Contempt threw the walking staff he was carrying to the ground. The staff writhed and twisted, singeing the ground in each direction before lying in a red-hot torpor.

Birds scattered, as fast as they could, to report to all and sundry to stay away. Other creatures scurried and hid. If the trees could have uprooted themselves, they would have.

The sorcerer had recently transformed his appearance. His hair now matched his pitch-black cloak, as did his fingernails. He liked his new look very much. He believed it made him appear dashing and refined. It did neither. It merely heightened his evil character. Unfortunately, he had only changed his outside appearance. His evil temper and ugly mood spread from his every pore, challenging the very air, which sizzled and spat as he walked. However he could not disguise his eyes; livid white, they fumed at the world.

'Come to me, walking wand!' he commanded his staff.

Still red at its centre, the staff hurtled through the air into his hand, where it whimpered in his grasp. The sorcerer crushed it in his fist until it ceased making any sound. 'That's better,' he growled in an oily voice, 'remember, you serve me and only me!' He closed his eyes and exhaled harshly.

'Interference! Interference by that lizard with wings! I brought the butterfly back to Wish and he steals her from under my nose! Argh, I hate those pesky dragons!' He peered at the world through slits of eyes, all the while muttering aloud. 'I wanted to put an end to that butterfly!' He strode for a while then paused and glared. Birds screeched and fled.

'Rainbow dragons!' he spat in another flood of hatred. 'That is twice too often one has ruined my schemes!' He stroked his chin. 'That will have to wait for now, my lovely,' he whispered to the walking staff in his grip. 'Yes, rainbow dragons will have to wait for another day.' With a hiss, he turned briskly and then stopped. 'What have we here?' he smirked.

As silently as a great dark ghost, the Sorcerer of Great

Contempt slithered behind a tree. The tree shuddered at his touch but the sorcerer ignored it. Absorbed, he watched intently then choked back a laugh. The staff he held whimpered at the sound, knowing there was no kindness in his mirth.

'So, a good day, after all,' the sorcerer grinned. 'Excellent! Come, let us embark.' Clutching his walking staff with an iron fist, he began to stalk stealthily through the forest.

...

Will was exhausted. His clothes were threadbare, and his shoes full of holes. Cold and hungry, he gazed weakly around. I'm lost, he thought sadly. He had just spent an aeon as a shrub, standing still. His legs had forgotten the business of walking.

'I hate it here,' he whispered. 'I hate this place. Why in blazes did I come here all those years ago?' At his feet lay a fallen branch. He picked it up. 'I want to go home,' he gasped. 'I want to go home.' Leaning heavily on the branch, he shambled on.

...

A chilling smile tarnished the sorcerer's face. 'So! Soon we will meet again, eh? He wants to go home! Perhaps to his Mummy?'

The Sorcerer of Great Contempt sniggered. 'The only problem there my friend, is that you've been here a long, long time. You have no home, you fool; everything you once knew is gone!'

His laughter caught the wind, swept through the trees, then froze and became still.

…

Will paused. Shivers crossed his sweating brow. Catching his breath, he peered around before glancing furtively over his shoulder.

'Is someone there?' he ventured uneasily. He shook his head at the eerie feeling. Agitated, he walked on. A dark shadow stalked his heart. Misery and despair crossed his soul.

'I'm lost!' he cried aloud. But there was no one there to hear or care.

CHAPTER 6

Insight

Candela stepped close to Coraggio as he peered into the pond.

'Are you sure?' she murmured. 'Are you sure it's best to summon the Oath? Perhaps you should try calling, one more time.'

Coraggio tossed his head. 'Yes, I'll try one last time.'

'Oobaat,' he thundered, 'Oobaat, this is no time to abandon those who need you!'

The forest sat on the shimmering edge of tension.

Rana's croak shattered the silence. 'Let me call him. Perhaps if I call, he'll come back.'

Coraggio had waited long enough. 'No, youngster,' he answered kindly, 'the Sorcerer of Great Contempt is growing stronger as we speak. We must fight him. We must all fight, as best we know how.' He shook his mane. 'We must start now.'

Rana crept closer to Coraggio. 'But why do you need Oobaat? He's just the gatekeeper to the wishing pond. Surely the mighty unicorns don't need help from him.'

The herd was moving, preparing to summon the Oath.

Rana was a persistent frog. 'Why would unicorns need, um, an old tortoise to help them fight something mean and bad?'

Coraggio ignored him.

Insistently, Rana crept under Coraggio's feet. He looked up with a puzzled frown.

'You've got your whole herd to help you get that sorcerer,' he implored. 'Oobaat's very, very old, you know. Perhaps it's too big a strain for him.'

Despite their preparations, and the dire situation, the herd began to giggle.

Rana looked around. 'Did I say something funny?' he asked.

The herd were tossing their heads and chortling, as if he were very funny, indeed.

'Well, did I?' he huffed.

The herd began to laugh in earnest. Even Candela smiled, as mighty Coraggio struggled for calm.

With a twinkle in his eye, Coraggio coughed. 'Enough, young frog,' he kindly snorted. 'We must prepare to summon the Oath, so please step away and find a safe spot somewhere else.'

Rana sighed. He knew there were no answers here. With an enormous bounce and a booming croak, he leapt away, resigned to watch.

'Frogs have no rights in this pond,' Rana grumbled crossly.

Without another word, the herd began to line the edge of the wishing pond. Soon they fully surrounded it, so where the ground and water met, a ring of unicorns stood with just their front feet getting wet. Silently, they stared toward the centre, their faces serious, in contemplation.

Rana's eyes stood on end. He hoped they weren't going to hurt poor Oobaat! With a whimper, he crawled under a lily leaf. From his hoped-for safety, he watched on.

In a penetrating whisper, Coraggio spoke:

With the moon that shines upon us
And the sun that comes each day
I call out; I call out to the heavens
With a summons and a prayer!

The entire herd dipped their horns briefly into the wishing pond. Immediately, the water churned and bubbled. Then, just as quickly, it became still. All was silent. The herd stood for what seemed a long time, unmoving.

'It must be over,' Rana muttered to himself. 'Well, that wasn't so bad.' He began to crawl out from under the leaf. Suddenly, though, he scampered back. There was *something* out there!

In a more commanding tone, Coraggio chanted:

From time begun
When thought was new
Lilifel and First Ones
Together grew

All knowing, all powerful
All seeing, all strong
So it was
Life began

Lilifel chose white
Hooves, manes and tails
First Ones chose hands and feet
But not Number One

With power earned
Of truth, of love
Lilifels call
Justice! Honour! Duty now!

For the greater good
Send us the one
The one who leads
Send us the One!

Coraggio stopped speaking. The herd waited. Time passed.
Rana peeked from his hideaway. 'This time,' he grunted, 'it must really be over!' He began to scratch and yawn, then stifled a squeak and hid again.

In one solid voice the herd recited:

Spirit, Fire, Air, Earth and Water
Moon, Stars, Sun and Sky
With the Staff of Life
All tasks are not done

Arise now
Number One
Arise now
The day has come

Lilifel
And First One
Forward together
A battle to be won!

The moon dimmed and the stars disappeared. A light crashed through the night sky then burst into flames. The earth thrashed beneath the herd's feet. It seemed as if the forest stopped breathing. Finally the ground settled.

Rana's eyes fairly popped from his head. His heart pounded so loudly it was all he could hear.

Suddenly, from the stillness, there was singing. It seemed to come from far away. With a jolt, the pond began to churn.

Rana squealed. Oobaat had returned! Oobaat the tortoise surfaced, and began to swim to shore. *But what was happening?* As terrified as Rana was, he couldn't tear his eyes away.

The air around Oobaat was thick with shifting colour and light that dissolved and sparkled as he moved. And then, in front of everyone's eyes, Oobaat's shape transformed, and he became a human! He left the pond and stood up.

With a sigh, the herd stepped away from the pond's

edge, but Coraggio stayed his ground.

For several silent heartbeats, the unicorn and man locked eyes.

'So, you did it. You really did it,' the man rasped.

'Yes,' Coraggio replied evenly. 'We need you Oobaat… and we need you like this.'

'In the shape of a man,' Oobaat choked, emotion thick in his voice. He held his human hands in front of him and gazed silently at them before turning and staring into his beloved pond. His reflection confirmed that it was true. He was indeed a man of human-kind with a dignified air and clothing to match. With a sigh, Oobaat turned to the herd.

'Well, this time you've really prepared me for battle! It looks like Lilifel and First Ones unite again for the cause of the outside world.' He shook his head. 'Ah, the hardest shape of all… to be a man.'

The herd stood quietly. Oobaat, their friend, was deeply sad.

Rana crawled out from under his leaf. What had happened to his dear mentor? What was all this about?

Fire in the sky, and stars that went out? Oobaat and First Ones? What was a First One? Lilifels? Were they really unicorns? And all this business of oaths and shape-changing, here, in the forest? What was meant by talk of battle? What was it all about?

Rana crept closer. His head spun with unanswered questions. Perhaps such strange things happened in Wish, but this was the forest where the rules shouldn't change. He shrank; they were talking again!

'Did you bring it?' Coraggio breathed, peering closely at Oobaat.

Oobaat nodded sagely. 'Yes, it was impossible not to. No First One summoned comes without their power.'

The herd shuffled.

From his side, Oobaat drew forward a long wooden cane.

The herd exhaled with relief.

'Ah,' Coraggio nodded.

For a brief moment each unicorn's horn glowed golden and then, just as quickly, paled.

'Yes, just as she always was,' Candela whispered into the pause. 'The *Staff of Life*, in all her glory.'

Oobaat pondered. 'How many are left, I wonder? Or is she the last one?'

In a gesture of deepest reverence, he held the staff close to his cheek. The Staff of Life briefly hummed.

Rana's eyes popped. *Power?* Once, Oobaat had threatened to make Rana disappear! Perhaps he hadn't been bluffing! Rana shivered. *Oobaat had power? He wasn't just a gatekeeper then?* Rana sat up with another thought. Oobaat had called himself a First One! What in blazes did he mean?

A rustle and a splash rang through the pond.

Oobaat and Coraggio glanced knowingly at each other.

'Rana the frog, you're eavesdropping!' Oobaat boomed. 'Come out from under that lily right now!'

Rana yelped. Oobaat, his dear mentor, was yelling at him, and he hadn't done anything wrong, for once! Remembering *powers*, Rana crept forward.

'Not there,' Oobaat commanded, 'come here, Rana.' He finished in a kinder tone. 'Please, don't be afraid.'

Rana wasn't sure what he was feeling. He *was* a bit afraid, but, for some strange reason, mostly sad. He hopped dutifully closer, and then slumped unhappily without looking at anyone.

Oobaat hunkered down. 'Rana,' he began kindly, 'Rana, I have a job for you.'

Rana's heart jumped. It was certainly Oobaat's voice! He looked up, despite his fears.

'That's better,' Oobaat smiled. 'Now, while I tell you this news, sit here in my hand.'

Rana crept, still downcast, onto the man's outstretched hand.

'Look at me, Rana,' Oobaat insisted.

Rana peeked at the man. His heart grew lighter. They were definitely Oobaat's eyes!

'Good, now listen carefully, little helper.' Oobaat instructed. 'While I'm away, and I'm not sure how long that may be, you will finally have what you've always wanted.'

Rana held his breath.

'Yes,' Oobaat smiled, 'I give to you, for the time being, the gatekeeper's duties of the wishing pond.'

Rana gaped in disbelief. His greatest dream had come true!

'Oh, Oobaat,' he roared, 'I promise I'll do a good job, and I promise I'll make you proud! Thank you! Thank you!' Rana could no longer contain himself and, with a huge bound, he plummeted back into the pond. 'You're mine, you're mine!' he boomed as he bounced from lily pad to lily pad. 'For a while, I'll be the boss around here!'

Oobaat and Coraggio looked meaningfully at each other.

'I hope I'm doing the right thing,' Oobaat grimaced. 'I never thought I'd see the day when I'd let him take charge of my important tasks.'

Coraggio nodded. 'He will manage,' he murmured thoughtfully. 'The frog will manage better than you might believe.'

Bemused, they watched Rana do a long-limbed colourful dance. Rana's bright red eyes and handsome orange hands and feet made wild gestures, as he puffed his blue chest out and flung his green body from leaf to leaf.

Oobaat winced. 'I hope so, my friend. I surely hope so.' He studied Rana thoughtfully before turning with resolve. 'Maybe you're right,' he finally murmured.

The herd shuffled. The moon was lifting clear of the sky. Daybreak was near. It was time to go. Lovingly, they looked around at their forest. Each one took a deep breath of its timeless air. A small shiver passed through their ranks. This was a rare and strange day indeed.

Wish… it was time for all unicorns to go to Wish!

CHAPTER 7

Venture to be

'We've drunk seven cups of tea,' Rielle frowned, trying hard to keep the impatience from her voice, 'so can we go now, please?'

Pud snored loudly and twitched in his sleep, his belly bloated with bread rolls and tea. Old slurped an eighth cup of tea as if it were his first.

'Out there,' Old muttered, 'out there, a whole world. Forgotten, long gone... other times.'

Rielle could hear only part of the things he said. She yawned and waited.

'Hope, if only... Hope,' Old continued. 'Must not forget... take *it!*' He gobbled another enormous slice of cake.

Where does all this cake come from? Rielle wondered. Each time she thought they might leave, Old would serve more tea and cake. Rielle knew she couldn't eat another bite. Politely, she tried to prompt the First One.

'Pud and I have to go soon.'

Old poured more tea. 'Long forgotten... paths... mountains... the bridge. Hope. Others maybe... more...

Old leave mountain... no... who knows... cannot be named... time.'

Rielle sighed. It wasn't as if she wanted to go to Wish. She hadn't liked Wish the first time she'd gone there. Her throat grew tight. *Perhaps by some wonderful chance, Far would be alright?* Anyway, Hope had to be told; it was the right thing to do. One thing was for sure, the tea seemed to have worked. She looked over at Number Twenty Three of the First Ones. He was drinking his tenth cup of tea. Rielle decided he must be terribly sad; he seemed to need an awful lot of tea for sadness.

Rielle... Rielle... Rielle!

Rielle jumped. 'Hooley dooley, did you hear that?' she gasped. 'It's that voice calling me, again!'

Old stopped eating. He cocked his good ear and listened. 'A voice calls to you,' he whispered, 'from places far away.'

'You heard it!' Rielle cried.

Pud sat up, shook hard and yawned.

Rielle looked at Old. 'I'm sorry, I don't want to be rude, but I'm going now, whether you're ready or not.' She wanted to thank the First One and be on her way, but Old jumped up from the table and quickly took her hand.

'Wait,' he implored, 'wait. I have drunk and I have eaten. So too have my guests. I am ready now. Wait, I have to bring *it* too.' His eyes pleaded with Rielle and his soft doeskin hand was warm and kind.

'Alright, I'll wait for a little minute.' Rielle found she couldn't deny the odd, kind creature.

Old nodded at her. 'Wait!' he called again before dashing from the room.

Pud scratched himself and sneezed.

Rielle's eyes fell on the cake tin. Intrigued, she stepped over to it and looked inside. It was empty. She was sure they'd eaten much more than it could ever hold.

Old rushed back. In his hand he carried something long and thin that was wrapped in golden cloth. Rielle didn't want to pry, but she was curious.

Timidly, Old glanced at Rielle. Then he walked around his little kitchen. His mouth drooped. He sighed; a big long sigh. He picked up the cake tin.

'Tea for sadness,' he muttered, 'tea for sadness must come too.' Putting a small sack of tea into the cake tin, and tucking the long, thin cloth-covered item under his arm, he went and gently took Rielle's hand.

'Once I used to climb the mountain,' he whispered, looking up at her, 'but then I went inside and I never saw the day.' He blinked and clutched his arm full of things, finishing the thought. 'But Hope is *Enin On, Number Nine of the First Ones*, and I must find my brother. That is law.'

Pud wagged his tail and nudged Old. Old wagged his tail and nudged Pud.

'Come, Rielle,' Old smiled sweetly. 'It is time we go to Wish.'

Like a small procession, Pud, Rielle and Old walked through his little parlour toward the entrance of the long, narrow passage. Old stopped and turned to look at his golden den one more time. Dropping Rielle's hand, he kneeled. Holding the gold-covered item in both hands, like an offering, he bowed.

'Keep the gold for time,' he breathed. 'Keep the gold for time.'

He stood up. Without another word, he clasped Rielle's hand again, and this time, Old led the way. As they walked down the passage and away from Old's den, sounds from outside the mountain began to boom and crash.

'It sounds like boulders are still falling down from the mountain-top,' Rielle whispered, worried.

'The mountain likes to chat,' was all Old replied.

Once again they skirted stalactites and dark, deep rock pools, until at last, they left the world of gold behind and strode outside the mountain into the night. The moon beamed a chalk-white light that reflected brightly off the canyon walls.

Old squealed at the unaccustomed brightness and covered his naked eye. Slowly, he peeked through the fingers of one hand, then, blinking hard, he let the moonlight in. Looking around at the outside world he sighed then smiled, and peered up at Rielle. Still holding her hand he began to turn and walk away.

'Where are you going?' Rielle quizzed.

'To the bridge, my little bridge, my little bridge that these hands made... that these hands made with fondness,' Old replied, tugging her forward.

Rielle tugged back. 'We can't,' she replied breathlessly. 'It's gone!'

Old stopped, looked back at her and kinked his mouth.

'Gone?' he asked, puzzled. 'Can't be gone, no such thing as gone, these hands built it fondly to last for time.'

Rielle shook her head hard. 'No, Old, the bridge broke. It broke when Pud and I came across the canyon.

We nearly didn't make it, as a matter of fact!'

Old gasped. 'The Bridge of the Long Forgotten, broke? Not possible,' he croaked horrified. 'Nothing can break the Truth of Time! The bridge was built with these own hands.' He dropped Rielle's hand and looked at his own hands as if he'd never seen them before; as if they weren't the hands he thought they were. Old looked up, puzzled. Doubt wrinkled his brow.

'Trouble! There is trouble!' he muttered, looking unsure which way to turn.

Rielle didn't have the heart to tell him that not only did his beloved bridge break, but it fell away into the watery abyss.

'It was just ancient,' she tried to assure him. 'It was just an ancient, unsafe, rickety bridge. It was bound to break sooner or later.' She grimaced at the memory. 'Bear's breath,' she swore, 'I'd have preferred it to break when I wasn't on it though!'

Old stamped a foot. 'No! Not ancient! No, not ricket-ee! No, no, *never* unsafe!'

Rielle was beginning to wonder about Old and his sudden outbursts. They were unsettling, to say the least.

He stamped his foot again. 'Trouble! There trouble! The Bridge of the Long Forgotten was protected by the *Truth of Time*. It looked ricket-ee but it could never break. That is the promise that I made!' With a rushed movement he put his cake tin on the ground and pulled the golden cloth away from the long, thin item he held.

Rielle was disappointed. It was just a wooden stick.

It had seemed much more mysterious when it had been covered up. Looking at Old uncertainly, she wasn't sure what to say.

'It's a walking cane,' she ventured.

Old snorted. 'Walking cane, my feet!'

Old tapped the stick. As he did so, the cane sang in a sweet, high voice.

Rielle gaped. She couldn't understand the words, but something told her they made perfect sense.

Old picked up his golden cake tin. Holding the stick as if it were indeed a lowly walking cane, he huffed off in the opposite direction to his once beloved bridge.

Rielle and Pud looked at each other, puzzled.

'What does it mean, faithful Pud?' Rielle whispered, but Pud glanced at the disappearing First One and, barking, ran to catch up with him.

'Charming,' Rielle sulked, 'just go and leave me behind. I was only telling him the truth. Wait,' she called after the First One, 'please wait. Remember we're both going to the same place!' Rielle caught up to Old and Pud.

'Thanks Pud,' she breathed sourly, 'just run off, why don't you? A huge boulder could have carried me clean over the cliff, and I doubt you would have cared or noticed.'

Pud sneezed, licked her hand, then pushed against her and looked up with a grin.

Reluctantly, Rielle patted his head. 'Alright,' she sighed, 'I forgive you. But don't leave me behind like that again.'

With his back up and his short legs pounding, Old stomped unhappily ahead. A stone wall ran beside the path, forming a protection from the cliff edge. It stood no higher than Old's head and lined the edge of the cliff in a carefully woven patina of rocks and boulders of all shapes, colour and size.

Old pointed at the wall, not looking back or left or right.

'This, too, I made with hands of fondness. This wall, the Serpent's Way.' He stomped on. 'It stands, it stays, no trouble here!'

'I'm sorry,' Rielle caught up to him. 'I'm sorry, Old. Perhaps it was the weight of Pud and I, but, well, but, the bridge was swinging so badly in the wind, and then it just simply fell apart.' She almost had to run to keep up.

Old said nothing.

'I think I should also be upset,' Rielle went on. 'When the bridge broke, it nearly took us with it.' She shuddered. 'We nearly fell into the river!'

Old stopped. For moments he remained silent.

'Not your fault,' he sighed at last, 'not anyone's fault.' He looked up clear-eyed at Rielle. Slowly, he raised the walking cane until he held it in both hands.

Rielle waited. The night was very still where they stood. The mountain listened, waiting for answers, and Pud sat at attention as if he owned a secret.

Old raised the stick and touched it. It briefly hummed.

Casting an ancient, otherworldly glow, the moon rocked gently above. All that the group could hear was the sound of their own breathing.

In barely a whisper, Old chanted into the waiting shadows:

In my hands
I hold the Wand of Time
I hold the Wand of Time
Things I make they cannot break
I hold the Wand of Time!

Old peered at Rielle from his uncovered eye.

'Good, Rielle,' he whispered, 'very, very good. Old is Number Twenty Three of the First Ones. I am Eerht ytnewt On. There is trouble, and it is time. I must find the others!' He smiled kindly at Rielle's fearful face. 'Come,' he urged, taking her hand, 'together we go to Hope.'

CHAPTER 8

When nightmares are true

Dizzy with effort, Will could not go on. He stumbled and then fell. Every muscle in his body ached from marching up hill and down dale. Hungry and cold, he lay dazed.

'She called me a villain,' he whimpered, 'she called me a villain. I'm *not* a villain,' he protested as his eyes clouded over. 'I wasn't a villain then, either. I just didn't know. I didn't know!' Will sobbed into the goose-down grass.

'I didn't mean to hurt the unicorn. I just wasn't thinking; it's true, it's true!' He tried to beat the grass with his fist, but his exhausted hand wouldn't move. 'I did my best to fix it,' he proclaimed. 'Yes, I did. I'm no villain. I'm not, I'm not.'

The sun departed in rich royal red, as a froth of pale evening floated in. Wish darkened and prepared for the night.

Will briefly opened his eyes. He stared bleakly at the darkening sky.

'Am I a villain?' he quietly asked. Staying where he lay, he pulled his cloak slowly around himself with the stiff movements of an old man. Then, his mind fading, he slid into restless sleep.

Like a streak of dark oil, a figure emerged from behind nearby trees. It walked slowly around Will as he slumbered.

'So,' the Sorcerer of Great Contempt breathed through clenched teeth, 'so, we meet again, Willful James.'

The walking staff in his grip whimpered.

'Hush my pretty toy,' the sorcerer hissed, clutching the walking wand even as it shuddered. 'Hush, or your days of singing will be over.'

A smirk etched on his features, the sorcerer continued to circle Will, occasionally prodding him with the staff. Buried in unnatural slumber, Will groaned. The night hung like heavy molten lead.

'Ah,' the sorcerer gloated, 'much time has passed since our first meeting.' He laughed; it was a greasy sound. 'Yes,' he reflected, 'too much time has passed here in Wish.' With an aim to chill the blood, he struck Will with the walking wand. Both Will and the staff moaned in despair.

The sorcerer bent over, pushing his face malevolently close to Will's. Will twitched, in deepest sleep, misery engraved on his face. Grinding his teeth, the sorcerer stood up. Breathing hard and trembling with rage, he beat the staff onto the ground.

'Because of you, you weak, wasteful coward,' he condemned Will, 'I have lost two glorious chances for escape from this place! Do you think you came to Wish all those years ago with a desire to kill a unicorn? You fool,

Willful James! That was not only your wish... *it was mine!*'

The sorcerer laughed chillingly. 'Why do you think I toyed with you? You were young and silly, a mere selfish boy. A spoiled prince, too full of his own wealth and charm! If it had been up to you, my friend, the first time I refused to help, you would *never* have returned.'

The night held its breath as if at long last it understood a tragic mystery.

'It was unicorns who trapped me here!' the sorcerer spat. 'It was unicorns that forced me to exile in Wish! Even my own kind turned against me... yes, they turned against me and between them all, I have been stuck here, ever since.' He raised his walking staff, as if to strike Will again, but changed his mind. Sour hatred coloured his voice.

'Because of you,' he glared, 'I also lost the precious reward of gold! Oh, I didn't need it for reasons you would understand. I don't need gold for trinkets and *things*.' He grimaced with contempt. 'Because of you, Willful James, both times I had a unicorn within my grasp, it escaped. The first time, it was the mother, and later, her son. I only need to kill *one* unicorn. Just one! That will be enough to damage the Ritual of Return.' Pensively, he looked around, crushing the staff in his hand. '*Wish* is the cage I'm in. I must escape from this place!'

Dark rage coursed through the veins in his temple. He poured that rage onto Will. 'You let your stupid heart interfere. At the eleventh hour, you showed yourself to be a coward! You wished! You fool! You became a shrub... a bush with magic leaves! You sacrificed yourself to save the she-unicorn, and then you sat there trapped for aeons, while the unicorn ran free!' The sorcerer ground his teeth so hard that his lip began to bleed.

'You will pay for your weakness, Willful James. No one crosses me! That you will see. Only a feeble-minded human could have so brilliantly spoiled my perfect plans!' He looked up, shaking his fist at the sweet, crisp night. 'This boy thinks he's the only one who hates this place. Hah! Wish! I have been trapped here for what seems like forever. *From the minds of humans, where anything is possible, except my escape!* Unicorns will pay for this. Yes, they will pay, and so will my own kind, those weaklings who let their minds be swayed.'

He pushed Will viciously with the staff. 'You,' he seethed, 'you weak, spineless creature. You will once more do my bidding, Willful James, and you will succeed so that I can win!' Will cried out, but slept on.

The sorcerer bared his teeth, his eyes glittering. 'This time boy, I have an extra little helper.' The walking staff he held sobbed quietly. The Sorcerer of Great Contempt sneered. 'I have managed to find this precious *stick*,' he mocked. 'Nothing will stand in my way again!' He struck the ground and was gone.

The moon crept out from behind a cloud. The night breathed a sigh.

Will stirred, but did not wake. The ground around him, though, was now an unfortunate, dark green, slimy sludge.

From the topmost branch of a tree, a large shadow loomed. It shuddered and then breathed a sigh of relief. Nodding as if it suddenly understood, it made sure it could not be seen, and then it flew away toward the Tower of Dreams.

Will slept a restless night long. Terrifying dreams plagued his mind. Just as the sun began tickling his face, he awoke with a startled shout. Clutching his cloak, he jumped up, panting hard. Twitching with fear, he glanced quickly around.

'Urgh,' he grimaced, his lip curling in disgust, 'it must have rained... the ground is thick with slime and mud.' He felt his clothes. *How can that be?* He wondered. *My clothes are dry!* Horrified, Will stared at the ground surrounding him. His heart trembled. Shivers crossed his spine. The mud lay around him in a slimy circle. Distraught but still weak, he urgently needed to escape its filth.

Leaping, he barely managed to land clear of it. Repelled but fascinated, he looked back. A shadow crossed his mind and the whisper of a dream scratched his thoughts. He almost understood something, like a distant memory, but then it was gone. Will frowned. He knew he was not faring well.

The sun flushed the morning with a breathless whisper and birds began to pipe and sing.

'Where to now?' Will asked himself half-heartedly. Squinting, he began to walk toward a sun-filled glade, clutching his cloak around him for warmth.

Psst!' someone called.

Will looked around. There was no one there.

'Psst, here!' the voice called again.

Will stopped. He wondered if it was just his mind.

'Psst! Psst! Psst!'

Will looked up. Far, the butterfly, was perched just out of reach.

Will scowled. 'Oh,' he continued to walk past, 'it's you.'

'Not just me,' Far piped, 'it's me returned!'

Will staggered and almost fell. His clothes hung on his shrunken frame and his hair hung limply beneath his hat. Smudged hollows darkened around his eyes and harsh lines cut his mouth.

'Go away,' Will slurred his words. 'You're no use to me.' Will stumbled. 'Can't you see I'm almost done for?'

'I can help you,' Far cried.

Will didn't care. 'Get lost, flutter-thing,' he snarled. 'I'm dying. It's over. I'm finished. It's too late now.' Will crashed hard to the ground. The sun dimmed and his world went dark.

'Flightlord, I need your help,' Far roared. 'We have to save him before he dies!'

Without a word, Flightlord swooped to the ground. He nudged Will, but Will could no longer speak. With one swift movement, Flightlord picked Will up gently, and held him carefully within his powerful jaws.

Far perched on Flightlord's nose. 'To the Tower of Dreams,' she cried. 'Hope will know what to do with a dying human!'

Incidentally let's transcend

Oobaat balanced the Staff of Life in both hands, like an offering. Taking a step toward the lip of the pond, he glanced kindly at Rana, who watched alertly.

'We won't need you, Rana,' Oobaat explained quietly. 'The herd and I will not be travelling to Wish, in the usual way.' Sensing Rana's disappointment, Oobaat searched for words to explain. 'When the herd do things as one, it binds them, much like the Ritual of Return. So, to go to Wish, all they need is to share the same thought.'

Rana blinked crossly. 'That would be right,' he muttered, 'I finally get the chance to let someone through the wishing pond and they don't need me after all.'

Oobaat's heart warmed despite the frog's unhappy face.

'There'll be plenty for you to do while I'm away, Rana.' He smiled. 'I promise you'll be busier than you think.'

Rana nodded obediently. 'Goodbye everyone,' he whispered as he turned and hopped away.

Once again, Oobaat raised the staff in both hands, and now the herd closed ranks. Anticipation nipped the air. Hush wandered with intent through the forest and lent itself to the unicorn's faces. All things rested on a pinnacle of purpose.

Commotion erupted. 'Wait for me, wait for me!'

Startled, the unicorns and Oobaat looked toward the uproar. Scuttling as fast as it could, an enormous snail slid down the path toward them.

'Wait for me! Wait for me!' the snail called again. Then, misjudging its way, it crashed with a thud into Oobaat's leg. 'So sorry,' the snail beamed happily, 'but if Benny's going to Wish, then he'll need me to go with him, of course!'

The snail peered up at Oobaat. He'd never seen the human before. He wondered who he was.

Oobaat and the unicorns barely had time to recover when the forest was in uproar again.

'Bibs, come back! Don't leave me behind!' Another snail scurried through the forest before sliding to a stop beside Bibs.

'Little Bobs, please don't shout.' Bibs grinned. 'I meant to tell you I was coming here, but I didn't have the time.' *Little Bobs*, his younger cousin, was always tagging along behind.

Panting hard, little Bobs tried to catch his breath. One day, he'd be big and strong just like Bibs, and it would be easy to keep up, no matter what.

The herd shuffled.

Oobaat looked sternly at the snails. 'Bibs and little Bobs, we didn't order any snails. We're very busy here right now!' *There was work to do! What were the snails trying to prove?*

Bibs frowned. He thought he knew the man's voice, but he'd never seen him before. He wondered who in blazes he was. He and little Bobs looked at each other, but little Bobs just shook his head.

Coraggio stepped forward. 'Benny won't need you this time, Bibs,' he rumbled. 'This time the entire herd will be with him.'

Both snails gasped. 'The entire herd?' Bibs wheezed. 'The whole herd? All of you? Each and every one of you? Not one of you will be left to stay in the forest?' He gaped at Coraggio. 'But the forest can't be without unicorns!'

Coraggio sighed. 'It's not the end of the world,' he stated. 'We don't intend to be gone forever.' He paused, went to speak but changed his mind.

'Benny won't need you,' Oobaat cut in. 'Please, step aside so we can continue our business.'

Bibs and little Bobs looked glumly at each other. Dismayed, they slid away to the edge of the forest.

Once again silence slid down like a curtain.

For the third time, Oobaat closed his eyes and balanced the Staff of Life in both hands, like and offering.

'Sing,' he breathed to the staff. 'Sing for life!'

A golden glow shimmered through the unicorns' horns.

At first, nothing happened. Then, softly, like a tremble of joy, the Staff of Life began to hum, before its voice soared.

From the centre of the pond, Rana watched on. His big red eyes grew round with emotion. His heart swelled. Suddenly, he wanted to be the best frog he could be!

Bibs and little Bobs glanced solemnly at each other.

Understanding they were witnessing something too big for them to comprehend, they sat huddled at the edge of the forest. Watching the man and the unicorns, they listened captivated as the Staff of Life sang its song.

With the moon that shines upon us
And the sun that comes each day
Call out to the heavens
With a summons and a prayer

When time was new
And thought was true
Unicorn and First Ones
Together grew

All knowing all powerful
All seeing all strong
So it was
Life began

With power earned
Of truth and justice
Honour
Duty strong

Spirit, Fire, Air, Earth and Water
Moon, Stars, Sun and Sky
With the Staff of Life
All tasks are not done

The day has come
A battle to be had, a battle to be won
Together forward
Unicorn and the One.

The song ended with a lingering hum, like a baby laid to rest.

Still trembling at the command of the staff's message, the snails gaped, aghast. *Oobaat, the Staff of Life and the unicorns were gone!* Speechless, the snails slid cautiously back to the pond's edge.

'Where are they?' Little Bobs whispered.

'I... I don't know. They said they were going to Wish, but it was so sudden.' Bibs whispered back. 'I think it was magic or something.'

'How could so many of them just melt?' insisted little Bobs.

'I think you mean vanish,' Bibs quipped, smiling.

Bibs remembered a time when he had been the youngest one, and others had been mean to him, so he was determined to be nice to the youngster. Seeing how frightened little Bobs looked, Bibs tried to explain.

'I don't think with unicorns it matters if there's one or lots of them.' He barely understood how it worked, so he chose his words carefully. 'I think they just do things because they can. Maybe that means if they really want to, they can disappear!'

Awed, little Bobs grinned feebly. 'Gee, if I could do that I'd get into all sorts of trouble.'

'You can stop whispering,' boomed Rana.

The snails jumped.

'Please don't sneak up on people,' Bibs growled, still sensitive from the morning's happenings. 'You could scare some of us to death with that voice of yours!'

Rana leapt closer. 'Hello Bibs,' he said, barely looking at him, 'who, may I ask, is your young friend?'

'I'm little Bobs!'

Rana frowned. 'What happened to the other Bobs; you know the one I mean. He was really, really old, grumpy and slow.'

'He's retired,' Bibs answered gruffly, glaring at the frog.

Rana glared back. They scowled at each other.

Little Bobs looked from one to the other. This wasn't fun!

A fly buzzed past Rana's nose. He caught it, swallowed and smacked his lips. 'So,' he huffed, 'what can I do for you now that you're here?'

'Do?' asked Bibs.

'Do!' Snapped Rana. 'I am the gatekeeper, here, after all!'

'I don't need anything,' Bibs drawled. 'I only came because I heard Benny was going to Wish. But it seems he won't need me. No one seems to need Imperial Guards anymore.' He turned abruptly and began to leave. 'Good day to you, Rana the frog,' he called over his shoulder. 'Have fun pretending to be the gatekeeper, *again*.'

'I'm not pretending!' boomed Rana.

Bibs rolled his eyes. Everyone knew that Rana was *always* pretending. He'd tried to pretend he was gatekeeper the last time Bibs was at the pond.

'Come on, little Bobs,' Bibs muttered, 'we don't have to listen to this.'

'I'm not pretending! I'm not pretending! I'm not, I'm not, *I'm not!*' Rana roared furiously across the water.

With graceful dignity, the snails slid away. Then suddenly, Bibs skidded to a halt, winking at his cousin. Little Bobs gazed open-faced at him, wondering what it meant.

'We'll show that frog,' Bibs began, 'we'll show him he can't fool us with his pretend!'

Little Bobs frowned. 'What do you mean?' he asked, puzzled.

Bibs checked over his shoulder. Rana was jumping around, booming as usual. 'Well,' Bibs grinned, 'let's trick the foolish frog. He's been pretending, for as long as I know, that he's the gatekeeper at this pond. '

Little Bobs shrugged, confused. This was all new to him.

Bibs snorted loudly. 'Rumour has it that Rana's tried it before when he thought Oobaat, the tortoise, wasn't around. Everyone knows that Oobaat's the gatekeeper to the wishing pond and that only he can let you in to Wish!'

Little Bobs looked over Bibs' shoulder. 'Where is the tortoise, then?' he asked.

'Oh, he's always about somewhere,' Bibs replied.

Little Bobs blinked. 'So what will you do?'

'Ah, what will we do, my little cousin,' Bibs winked. 'Come with me; watch and learn!'

Promptly, he turned and began sliding back to the pond. With full faith in his older cousin, little Bobs followed.

Rana watched them approaching. He stopped bouncing and waited.

Reaching the pond's edge, Bibs paused. Locking eyes, he and Rana scowled at each other.

Little Bobs sighed. *Not this again,* he thought.

'So,' Bibs began, 'so, if you aren't pretending, perhaps you should let us go to Wish?'

Bibs grinned inwardly. That would show the frog! He had heard that Rana had let Rielle and Pud through the wishing pond once, and rumour told that Oobaat had punished Rana in all sorts of horrid ways. Bibs held back a chuckle. There was no way Rana would do it again!

Rana hopped closer to the snails. 'You want to go to Wish?'

Bibs smirked. 'That is what you say you do, isn't it? You know, as part of your gate-keeping duties?' He grinned at the frog.

'Are… are you sure you want to go to Wish?' Rana stammered, confused.

Bibs noticed his hesitation. 'Of course,' he quipped casually, 'why not?'

Rana was curious, but Oobaat had invested him with this important task, and he must fulfil it, no matter what. It was not the gatekeeper's place to make judgements. The gatekeeper simply recorded who passed through and let those seeking, know the rules.

'Is it just for you, Bibs?' Rana queried.

'It's for me *and* little Bobs,' Bibs replied, as he looked around for Oobaat to show up.

'I didn't hear the unicorns say they needed help from Imperial Guard snails,' Rana muttered, perplexed, 'so why would snails want to go to Wish?'

Bibs and little Bobs said nothing.

Rana shrugged, but his heart fluttered. He cleared his throat. This was his first official request, and even though it was an odd one, it was important to get it right. In a loud voice he began to fulfil the gatekeeper's duties, reciting the words that he'd been taught.

'As gatekeeper to this wishing pond, it is my duty to record the reason why you are going to the land of Wish,' Rana cited.

Bibs thought Rana was taking himself too seriously, but he continued to play the game.

'We want to go for the adventure,' Bibs replied, even as he winked at little Bobs and peered around for Oobaat.

Rana nodded and said sternly, 'Many venture to this gate, wishing this and wishing that. Although I guard the gate, I have no power to stop your wishes, give advice, or change your thoughts in any way, as that is not my place. All I do is record your presence, your reason for going, and the time and date.'

He paused, secretly proud of himself; it had taken a long time for him to remember the words. He continued.

'As you may or may not know, wishing is a tempting thing. It's quite a delicate business when you think about it, as wishes can be tricky things.' He took a deep breath.

'A wish often comes from your mind, but a dream always comes from your heart, and the easiest way to know the difference, is what you get from it in the end.' He frowned. 'It is clearly stated in lore that one must be very careful what is wished for. One must be clever and think it through, for if it comes from the mind, and not from the heart, then it isn't the right thing for you!'

Rana peered at Bibs and little Bobs. 'Are you ready to go then?' he checked.

Bibs looked around. Any minute now, Oobaat was certain to turn up and yell at Rana to behave.

'Yes, yes... we're ready,' Bibs declared. *Where on earth was the tortoise?*

'Wait then,' Rana urged. He jumped away and landed on an enormous purple water lily. Carefully, he propelled it directly to the banks of the pond. With a mighty bounce, he leapt onto the lily's centre and watched intently as the flower began to open.

'Now listen, carefully,' Rana roared, 'for I must tell you this. No matter what happens you must have faith, and if you feel you want to fret, I ask you to be strong, be true, believe and trust; be brave and never doubt!' Then he leapt free of the flower and called out to them. 'Jump on the flower's centre and you'll soon be off!'

Bibs and little Bobs looked at each other. *Where was Oobaat the tortoise?* Bibs wasn't sure what to do, but he couldn't turn and run away now!

'Come on little Bobs,' he whispered, 'the tortoise will be here to stop this any second, you'll see.'

And, so saying, Bibs slid onto the lily. With open trust and faith, Little Bobs followed his older cousin. Onto the centre of the lily they went, but of course, Oobaat never came. A gush of water rushed up to meet them. They were sucked into the vortex and snatched away.

CHAPTER 10

Goozey Boozey

'I don't know what Hope looks like,' Rielle puffed, as she tried to keep up with Old. The First One just kept walking, the Wand of Time clutched firmly in his hand. Pud trotted between them like a black bouncing ball.

'It's a long story,' Rielle tried to explain. 'I need to tell Hope I've lost something that isn't mine.' She glanced at Old. It appeared he wasn't listening.

'You see,' she continued, almost running to keep up with him, 'the same wind that shook us so horribly on the bridge, um, well, it also snatched Hope's butterfly and carried her away. Far, that's her name, was keeping Pud and I company while I searched for my dream.' She glanced at Old again.

His mouth was grim as he powered on. 'Trouble,' he muttered. 'Trouble took your little friend!'

'But it was just the wind,' Rielle answered unsurely. 'The canyon back there was not very friendly, after all.'

Old shook his head. 'Not canyon! Not mountain! Not little friend! *Trouble!* Only trouble can break the Truth of Time. Only trouble breaks things I build with these hands!'

The mountain path began to lead them down into the lowlands.

Rielle sighed. It had taken Pud, Far and herself what seemed like ages to climb the mountain, and now they had to go all the way back down again.

Had they done all that climbing for no good reason?

Rielle peered curiously at Old. He was walking with one hand placed tenderly on Pud's head as Pud gazed up at him with adoring eyes. Then, in a brisk movement, Old moved his eye-patch over to cover his other eye. Rielle was bursting to ask him why. She walked on silently for several strides, but at the risk of being impolite, she just had to know.

'Why do you wear the eye-patch?' she stammered. 'I… I mean both of your eyes seem fine, but you shift it from one to the other. Do they get sore or something?'

Abruptly, Old stopped. Carefully, he rested the cake tin and the walking wand on the ground. Then, with both hands, he lifted the eye-patch from his face and held it almost gently. He gazed down at the small black cloth, cradling it as if it were precious. He peered up at Rielle. Pensively, he smiled.

'I only have to see with part of me,' he whispered, 'and it is easier that way.' Then promptly, he replaced the eye-patch over one eye, collected his things, and walked ahead. Rielle and Pud watched him go.

Following on behind, Rielle watched Old's back. He seemed terribly alone. Her heart bled for the First One and she began to understand why Pud loved him so.

As they rounded a bend, the Serpent's Way ended and so did the night.

The first sunlight of the day washed them with sincere

colour and warmth, as bold orange splashes cloaked the valleys and lowlands. Old gasped and stood gazing at the spectacle, his hands clasped together in rapt delight. He blinked his bare eye rapidly, but it seemed to be coping well with the brightness. Under his arm, the wand softly hummed.

With reverence, Old drew the Wand of Time from the scrap of golden cloth. Its yellow wood glistened in the sun. Fondly, as if it were a child, Old whispered something to the stick he affectionately held, and the wand's voice promptly leapt to sing.

Spirit, Fire
Air, Earth and Water
Moon, Stars
Sun and Sky

The Truth of Time
We go seeking
Destiny
We will be meeting

Above, below
Beneath, beyond
Beyond the surface
Beyond the surface

Above
Beyond
Beneath
Below.

The sun rose fully over the horizon, bathing the group in a flood of tender pink. They paused, enraptured by the wand and its haunting song.

Rielle... Rielle... Rielle...

Rielle shivered. The voice seemed closer!

'What do you think it is?' she gasped to Pud and Old. 'What do you think it is?' A shudder of the unknown crept along her neck.

The sun flushed them with a darker colour, turning the three of them into statues of red. For a breathtaking minute their world stood still.

'Run!' Old called, breaking the silence. 'Run! There is trouble!'

Before Rielle could question him, a roar of upheaval thrashed from above and beyond them on the mountainside. She looked back. Two gigantic boulders were hurtling toward them. In that swift glance, Rielle could have sworn a sinister shape was pushing them.

Deafened by the boulder's fierce journey, the trio fled.

Rielle was amazed at how fast Old ran. He flung his short legs over rocks and jutting ground, leaping logs and twisted stumps as easily as Pud. With fear chasing her, she did her best to keep up.

Looking back to check on his mistress Pud barked abruptly. Without a word Old turned, and in one swift movement, he scooped Rielle onto his back and continued to run.

'Too slow!' Old called to her above the roar and din. 'The Truth of Time will carry you!' Still clutching the wand and the cake tin under one arm, Old galloped on, as if Rielle wasn't there.

Rielle gasped at the speed of the First One. He ran so fast that her teeth rattled and her vision blurred. She shut her mouth and closed her eyes tightly. Clutching him around his sturdy shoulders, she let Old carry her into the valley below.

Down the mountain they raced, streaking through the orange sunrise like tiny pebbles thrown by giants. Behind them the ground shuddered and crumbled where the boulders landed and rolled, crushing uneven dents into innocent ground.

They were almost on the flat of the lowlands where forest stretched towards them. With a last mighty surge, Old and Pud pelted into the thick of the forest, as ancient trees reached out to greet them.

The massive boulders swerved behind them to land in the nearby river; the booming of their ending reaching deep into the forest.

Promptly, Old let Rielle down off his back. She wobbled over to a log and sat on it. Pud lay down, panting. Puzzled, Rielle noticed that Old wasn't in the slightest bit short of breath.

'The boulders went into the river,' Rielle wheezed. 'They just swerved, as if they couldn't come in here.'

Old tenderly touched a tree. The wand hummed and the tree rustled.

'The forest is safe,' he smiled, as if he were greeting a long-lost friend.

'Yes, we're back in the forest,' Rielle murmured wistfully, 'we're almost back where Pud and I began.'

Squinting, she looked through the trees. Impossibly

far away, the mountain looked serene and untouchable. *We went all that way*, Rielle mused, *just to come straight back here.* She sighed and poked at a bruise on her leg, where she'd been bumped galloping down the mountain.

'I wonder if I will ever find my dream?' she murmured.

Old sniffed the air. 'No time for sorry,' he grunted. 'Trouble chased us down the mountain, and trouble sits upon our backs. Where is Hope, I ask?'

Rielle held back a shiver and hesitated before answering.

'We have to go to Wish,' she replied half-heartedly. 'Hope lives in the Tower of Dreams, and the tower is in Wish.'

Pud stood and shook himself. He barked several times and then trotted off, not looking back. Old followed the dog.

This time Rielle didn't get angry. She forged on to catch up with them.

'We need to find the wishing pond,' she insisted as she caught up with Old. 'It's the only way we can go to Wish. Well, the only way that I know of.'

Old nodded. 'Wish... yes,' he muttered under his breath, 'perhaps we will regret this Wish.' He sighed and stopped, then sniffed the air and put his good ear to the ground. 'Water and ponds lie there,' he pointed.

Through the hush of the forest, they trekked past a grove of tightly woven undergrowth and stepped around an enormous boulder that sat in the centre of the stony path.

'This is it!' Rielle cried, remembering the way.

With one thought, the three of them began to run. They rounded a gigantic ancient white tree that stood like a monument from another time, and there, on the other side of it, was the wishing pond!

The pond's mists drifted mysteriously before letting the visitors through. Rana leapt keenly to meet them, eager and happy with his important new job.

Rielle gaped angrily, skidding in her tracks. 'Hooley bondooley,' she exclaimed, 'not you again.'

Rana blinked up at her. 'Hello Rielle,' he croaked almost shyly, 'I promise this time I will tell you the truth.'

'You promised that last time!' Frowning, Rielle turned her back on the frog. 'Oobaat,' she called, 'Oobaat, where are you?'

Old struck the ground hard with his walking wand. Caught unawares, everyone looked at him, surprised. The forest shifted as if also commanded.

'You said Oobaat?' Old hissed.

Rielle felt one of his strange moods coming on. 'Yes,' she agreed uncomfortably, 'Oobaat the tortoise. He is the gatekeeper to the wishing pond.'

Old was holding his breath. His good ear turned red and his uncovered eye bulged. He giggled oddly, then laughed, clapped his hands, wagged his tail and jumped up and down.

'Hoo, hoo, ha, ha,' he squealed, 'at last, at last!'

Rielle, Pud and Rana watched curiously as Old laughed so hard that he was soon lying on the grass, holding his stomach and shaking his head. He jumped up and hugged Rielle with all the strength of his steely arms, leaving her gasping. Quickly, he stepped back. Glancing up, he saw the look on Rielle's face, but instead of explaining, he did a little dance. Then sharply, he turned to Rana with a no-nonsense look.

'Oobaat,' he rumbled, 'Oobaat. Where is Oobaat?' he barked.

Rana faced Old with all the sincerity he could muster. Oobaat had been right. There certainly was plenty to do in this job! He glanced pleadingly at Rielle and Pud.

'I promise this time I'm telling the truth,' he whispered. 'It's true when I tell you Oobaat isn't here. Oobaat has left me in charge of his duties, because as far as I know,' he gulped, 'he's gone... gone to Wish for a while.'

Old clapped his hands, a look of concentration on his face. 'Trouble!' he called. 'I say trouble! I am right!' He turned to Rielle and Pud. 'Come, we must find trouble!'

Rielle held back. 'But,' she began, 'how do we know Rana's truly being honest? Last time I was here he told me a lie. He let me go through without the gatekeeper knowing, and that's against all the laws.'

Old lifted his eye-patch, sniffed the air and squinted at Rana. Rana stared fearlessly back.

'No time to lose, Rielle,' Old boomed. 'The frog does not lie and we have trouble to find!'

Pud barked and covered Rielle's foot with his paw. He looked up, licked her hand and then sneezed.

'Hurry,' Old called to Rana, 'we go to Wish to find trouble!'

Urgently, Rana began reciting the rules. He finished the final words in a rush.

No matter what happens you must have faith
And if you feel you want to fret
I ask you to be strong, be true
Believe and trust
Be brave and never doubt!

Old clamped his half-moon mouth and tapped his toes impatiently.

'Yes, yes, yes! Old has lived! Old has heard! Old was here before you were born! Now hurry, little frog, send us away!'

Rana propelled the purple lily over to them then watched keenly as they scrambled on. At first, nothing happened.

Old looked up at Rielle and gently took her hand.

'You see, you goozey boozey,' Old kindly grinned, 'the mountain you climbed was not wasted. The Truth of Time brought you there. You chased your heart for a purpose.'

Before Rielle had a chance to ask him what in blazes a goozey boozey was, the water rushed up and sucked them in.

So it was that Old, Rielle, Pud and the Wand of Time went to Wish.

CHAPTER 11

Tell no lies or fly Far fly

'You're a villain, a villain, a villain!' A dark figure dressed in black called to Will. 'You're a villain!' The figure laughed. 'A villain, just like me!'

The figure lifted Will without touching him, and then flung him away to fly without wings. Will tried to run, but his tormentor caught up. Glaring, it blocked Will at every turn.

'You can't run, Willful James,' it shrieked, 'you can't run! Nothing can run away... from me!'

Frantic, Will tried to call out, but his voice was flimsy and useless in his throat.

'You are weak,' his tormentor called. 'You are a weak, spineless creature. You don't deserve to live! You don't deserve to live!'

Flinging an arm up to protect himself, Will recoiled and fell to his knees.

The dark figure loomed over him and pointed. 'Coward!' it cursed. 'Coward!'

Will's heart broke. He knew it was true.

. . .

Inside the Tower of Dreams, Hope stood and faced a knock at his door.

'Enter,' he beckoned.

Flightlord stepped into Hope's room. Carefully, as if Will might break, he eased Will from his powerful jaws and placed him on a bench. With a nod to Hope, Flightlord retreated.

With calm, elastic strides Hope reached Will. Bending his considerable height over the barely breathing young man, he placed one hand on Will's forehead and the other over Will's heart.

Far, the butterfly, circled Will frantically, looking for signs that he might still be alive.

'Shush Far,' Hope implored, 'shush. Be still and calm like I've shown you before. Let me check this unfortunate young fellow.'

Outside, standing by the windows of Hope's room, Flightlord stood guard. His great yellow eyes pierced the landscape for signs of dark shadows or things stranger than usual.

Hope mumbled something that Far couldn't hear, but she saw the look of disquiet in his eyes. Muttering vigorously, Hope placed both hands over Will's heart.

'I don't deserve to live,' Will groaned, 'I don't deserve to live.' A fresh flush of fever beaded his brow.

Hope made a decision. He bent closer to Will and began to croon:

Forgive
Forget

The past is done

Forgive
Forget
The harm has run

Forgive
Forget
Let go the pain

Forgive
Forget
No more self-blame

Forgive
Forget
Rest now rest

Forgive
Forget
Let your heart be free

Forgive
Forget
Let your spirit be!

As he finished his song, a ball of blue light leapt from Hope's hands, to fully surround Will. Will whimpered and thrashed. Punching the air as if fighting an invisible foe, he kicked and squirmed, calling out again and again.

'I don't deserve to live! I don't deserve to live! Leave me alone! I'm a villain, can't you see?'

As if it were competing for time, the blue light raced around Will. No matter what Will said or did, it pulsed brightly over him.

'Be still, young man,' Hope insisted. 'Let your spirit be!'

Will became motionless. The blue light grew paler, until at last it went white. Will began to breathe regularly then, but sweat poured from his every pore, leaving him drenched from head to feet.

Hope spoke to Far as if nothing had happened. 'His clothes will need laundering, I feel,' is all he said.

'His name is Will,' Far whispered, 'that's what he told me.'

Hope simply nodded.

Fluttering aimlessly, Far turned to Hope. 'Is it my fault?' she asked sadly. 'Should I have helped him first? I really needed to tell you about Rielle. I thought, well, I thought *that* was the most important thing!'

Hope looked fondly at the butterfly. 'Shush *farfalla*,' he scolded kindly, 'of course you did right. Rielle was your first thought, and duty of care, so stop fretting and put your mind to rest.'

Hope left Will's side and strode to Far. She was sitting slumped, with a worried look on her tiny face. Hope scooped her up until she looked straight into his eyes. Warmly, he smiled at his dearest charge.

'Of course you did the right thing. Rielle still needs your help to find her dream.' Hope's eyes became pin-pricks of seeking. 'However,' he continued in a knowing voice, 'the way you returned to Wish is most unusual. I dare not risk sending you out there again, until I understand what we are dealing with.' Gently, he placed Far down.

Turning swiftly, he called out. 'Flightlord! Flightlord, I need a portion of fermented moat mud. Would you be so kind as to fetch me some? Make sure it's very sticky and dark and chunky, if you please.'

Will shuddered, took a deep breath and groaned, but only his eyelids flickered.

'Good, he's still alive then,' Hope said matter-of-factly. He promptly threw the moat mud Flightlord handed him into massive pots on his windowsill. The pots brewed there with no visible fire.

Hope smiled at Flightlord's curious gaze. 'Protection!' is all he said. The rainbow dragon nodded and returned to his watch.

As she had done so many times, Far studied Hope as he began his healing.

Hope half closed his eyes. Holding his hands out, he declared in a commanding whisper:

Fever and Woolly Betony go hand in hand
Joepye Weed for clammy face
Elecam, elecam, elecampane
Gobble germs, make them go
Betony of Wood to chase the woe
A teensy pinch of Butterfly Weed
For coughs that hurt and make one wheeze.

One by one, the herbs and flowers that Hope needed appeared in his hands. Hope smiled, well pleased.

'Aahh!'

Hope and Far spun around. Will was staring at them with dread on his face. Hope stepped towards him but Will cringed in fear.

'Aahh! Get away from me! Get away from me!' Will croaked. He struggled to raise himself but found he couldn't. Weakly he fought his spinning head, but he was too ill to move.

'I will not harm you, Will,' Hope declared sincerely.

'Who are you?' Will gasped in a sickened whisper.

Will didn't wait for Hope to answer. 'You,' he choked, his breath raw and rasping in his throat, 'you're that evil sorcerer aren't you? I saw what you just did, making things appear in your hands. Only he can do that!' A fit of wheezing turned his lips greyish blue. Will closed his eyes. A memory of a dream stirred in his mind. He shuddered and prepared for the worst.

The blue light began to dance around Will again, growing darker and then lighter, as if it fought Will's deep, dark thoughts.

Hope waited, then nodded. Making sure Will's eyes were shut, he flung the plants and herbs he still held in his hands into pots of different coloured liquid. Hope turned. Will was watching him.

Hope stood tall and locked eyes with Will. 'You can fight me, young man,' he said unflinchingly, 'or you can help me make you well. Which is it to be? The choice is yours.'

Will grimaced at Hope's stern gaze. 'Everybody hates me,' he whispered. 'I turn everyone away.'

Hope waited for a proper answer. 'I intend to make

you better, Will,' he insisted, 'but it will be easier if we are in agreement about it.'

Will opened his eyes wide in surprise. 'Who are you?' he demanded. 'How do you know my name? Who are you that you should care about me?'

Hope paused before answering. Then, as if making a bold decision, he drew his brown hood away from his face.

'I am Enin On,' he declared, as if daring unseen forces to doubt his words. The blue light blazed around him. 'But to you,' Hope finished kindly to the shivering Will, 'I am Hope, just Hope... simply Hope. That is all you need to know, young man.'

Will's feverish eyes flushed with new emotion. 'Hope?' he asked weakly, as he began to fade. 'Hope? The flutter-thing didn't lie then?' Will gasped for breath. 'I... I mocked her... I didn't believe you were real, and then later, later, I told her to go away. I didn't believe, I didn't believe.' He shut his eyes. 'Where am I?' he whispered. 'Where is this place?'

Hope replied gently. 'This is the Tower of Dreams, Will.' He paused. 'And you are still in Wish.'

That was enough for Will; he promptly fainted.

'He's too ill to deal with anything.' Hope pondered. 'Tell me again, Flightlord,' he called to the rainbow dragon, 'tell me again, what you saw.'

Flightlord put his head inside the open window. It was easier that way. Hope's chamber inside the tower was far too small for several visitors at a time.

'I saw the Sorcerer of Great Contempt,' Flightlord began eagerly, but even as he said it, he checked over his shoulder to make sure it was safe to speak.

Hope nodded, encouragingly. 'The sorcerer can't come inside the Tower of Dreams, Flightlord,' he assured. 'That is impossible for him to do. But you are right to keep an eye out, for I have seen him occasionally sneaking by the moat.'

Far flew to sit on Hope's shoulder, where she knew she would be safe.

Flightlord recounted. 'I saw the sorcerer mumbling and cursing over that sleeping young man.' The dragon was afraid of nothing, but he shivered at the evil memory. 'I only heard pieces of what the sorcerer said, but I understood one thing. That young man is only partly to blame for the day he shot the female unicorn, long ago!'

Hope sat down, his eyebrows furrowed. 'Yes,' he breathed, 'yes, I fear it torments him. Tell me the rest of what you know.'

'The day I brought Far back to the Tower of Dreams,' Flightlord continued, 'she mentioned meeting a lost young man, but urgency demanded that she come straight here to you.' He checked over his shoulder again. The landscape was bare.

'Later, quite some time later, on one of my ventures, I was sitting peacefully in a high tree when I saw the sorcerer appear on the ground far below. He began to curse and babble but the young man slept on, unaware that he was there.' He paused.

'I waited and watched and listened, and finally the sorcerer went away. I wasn't sure what I should do, so I raced back to the tower and fetched Far. Together we flew to the forest, where we found Will awake. He was distraught and delirious. Just as Far and I reached him, he collapsed, so Far begged me to carry him here to you.' Flightlord finished with a shake of his head.

Hope nodded his thanks and stood. Turning from Far and Flightlord, he gazed outside at the almond orchards. For a long while he stared with wistful brooding in his eyes. Finally, he made a decision.

Striding to the far corner of his humble chamber, Hope stopped in front of an ancient chest made of light, honey-coloured wood. It had no visible lock or latch. Quickly, as if fearing he might change his mind, he kneeled. Holding one hand over the chest, he hastily stated a word, as if having made the decision, there was no time to lose.

'Ompri.'

The lid of the chest released without a sound. Hope opened the lid wide and peered in. With the serious face that Far was accustomed to, Hope reached inside. Carefully, as if it might break, he lifted something out. When he stood, he held the world locked in his eyes. The chest clicked shut as silently as it had opened. Hope took his prize to the middle of the room, holding it in both hands as if it were an offering.

Triumphantly, he looked up. In a voice struck with vision, he softly spoke.

'My friends... I hold before you, the *Wand of Faith!*'

CHAPTER 12

For the low places and the high

'Arrrggg!' spat little Bobs. 'Eeeaakkk!' spluttered Bibs. 'Arrggeeaak!' they both screamed as they shot from the water and landed on a sandy shore.

'It was easier last time,' Bibs complained loudly. 'It was much easier when Oobaat gave us a ride to Wish!'

Little Bobs was out of control. Rolled up tightly in his shell, the force of the landing sent him spinning like a coiled spring. He careered down a slope and landed with a thud into Bibs. Their shells made a loud crack as they collided, and for a while they both saw stars.

'Are you alright, little Bobs?' Bibs finally whispered.

'I fig I lunded ubsiddowd,' little Bobs replied.

'You think you landed upside down?' Bibs asked.

'Yeb,' answered little Bobs.

Bibs poked his face outside his shell. Yes, indeed, his young cousin was the wrong way up. 'Wait on, little Bobs,' Bibs cried, 'I'll see if I can fix it. Just give me a minute!' Bibs pushed and shoved, panted and puffed, but he couldn't shift the younger snail.

'Hubby dup!' called little Bobs, who was beginning to feel ill.

'I *am* hubbying, I mean hurrying,' Bibs exclaimed, 'but your shell's all stuck in boggy sand.'

'Yor bolt am ere,' little Bobs grunted, 'yub hubby n git mib oub ob ere.'

'Don't worry,' Bibs panted, 'I know it's my fault you're here. I'll get you out in a second!' But Bibs never got the chance to pull little Bobs out. Suddenly, water was rushing all over them as they were joined by others on the shores of Wish.

'Arrk!' Rielle spat water and landed on her feet. Pud yelped, did a somersault and then stood up, soaked. Old, however, walked with quiet dignity onto the shore, holding his walking wand and his cake tin still neatly tucked under one arm.

'Geb me oubt!' yelled little Bobs, as more water rushed into his upside down shell.

'Help! Help!' Bibs rushed up to Rielle. 'Help! Little Bobs needs help!'

'Bibs,' Rielle asked, amazed, 'is that you? What in hooley dooley are you doing here?'

'Tell you later,' Bibs puffed. 'You have to help save little Bobs! Quick,' he cried, 'or soon he'll drown!'

Rielle and Pud raced after the snail.

'Geb me oubt! Geblub, meblub blout!'

Reaching little Bobs, Rielle kneeled and, carefully but promptly, picked him up with both hands and turned him around.

'Bleeerrb!' Little Bobs was not amused, as a rush of salty water poured over his head. He gave a huge shake and then opened his eyes wide. A girl human! He'd never seen so many humans in one day!

'Thangub,' he called politely to Rielle. Then, seeing Bibs, a thunderous look crossed his face.

'You!' he roared at Bibs. 'You said tortoise, but no tortoise came! You said safe, but I nearly drowned! You said game, but it's no fun! You said you'd look after me 'cause I'm the younger one!' Little Bobs tore after Bibs who pelted away as fast as he could.

Rielle shook her head, puzzled. 'What do you think they're doing here, Pud?'

Pud was busy. He had something wet stuck up his nose.

'Somehow I don't see the snails needing to be in Wish, especially on their own,' Rielle muttered, shrugging her shoulders. 'I suppose they must have a reason for being here. It's just that last time they came to help Benny, as Imperial Guards. I wonder why they're here, now.'

Pud nudged Rielle hard. They had no time to lose, and his nose was fine now. He sneezed happily then urged her on.

'Oh well,' Rielle said, patting the dog, 'I'm sure they know what they're doing.' Untangling her soggy clothes and hair, she heard the snails shouting as they disappeared over the horizon.

'I hope you know what you're doing,' little Bobs hollered. 'You had better get us out of here!' Bibs bolted, hoping little Bobs would soon get tired.

Old pointed. 'We go that way,' he stated calmly, as if it were every day he got thrown on strange beaches where snails argued noisily.

'How can you tell?' asked Rielle, as she stood by him in her rapidly drying clothes.

Old held up the Wand of Time. A glow lit the honey wood. The wand strained in Old's hand, pointing east.

'She seeks her *own* kind,' Old whispered.

'Do you mean Hope?' Rielle asked, puzzled.

'Not Hope,' Old answered, 'her *own* kind.' He looked up at Rielle with an eye clouded in mystery.

'Who then?' Rielle persisted.

Old began walking toward the east.

'Who?' Rielle asked again.

Furtively, Old looked about. 'Come close. We will speak quietly,' he breathed. 'Wish is a place of much regret.'

Big-eyed, Rielle and Pud scuttled to be close to the First One.

'Who?' Rielle whispered under her breath, suddenly longing to be safe in Old's den, drinking tea and eating cake.

'*It's your fault and you know it!*' Over the rise of a hill the two snails rushed straight towards them.

'I *said* I know it's my fault,' Bibs yelled back, 'and I promise I'll make it up to you! The frog wasn't *supposed* to let us in. That isn't his job! It's never been his job! The tortoise will be furious when he finds out!'

Little Bobs didn't care. 'I want to go home,' he whimpered. 'I didn't want an adventure. I love the forest. I want to go home. I want to go home! I want to go home!'

Bibs stopped. Little Bobs skidded past him, turned around and, teary-eyed, paused.

'There's only one small problem with that,' Bibs considered.

'What?' little Bobs sniffled, forgetting the chase.

'I don't know how to tell you this,' Bibs answered quietly, 'but here goes. Um, without help from the tortoise, I have no idea how to go back home.'

Little Bobs went very quiet. 'Do you mean we have to stay here forever,' he finally snuffled, trying to be brave, 'until we're ancient and shrivelled and nearly dead?'

Bibs wasn't sure. 'No, no,' he answered, 'I don't think it will be quite that long. I'm sure, really, very sure that we can work out what to do. I mean, how hard can it be? We probably just go jump in the ocean or something, and then get sucked back into the bit that takes us home.'

'Let's try that then,' little Bobs agreed, cheering up and sliding on.

Bibs shook his head. 'But, on the other hand,' he muttered as he joined him, 'if that doesn't work, what will we do?'

Fully absorbed in their conversation, the snails weren't watching where they were going. Old struck his walking wand on the ground, and with a startled jump, the snails looked up.

'Imperial snails and too much talk!' Old frowned.

Bibs stared open-mouthed. Then, he said a very strange thing. 'Bow!' he breathed to little Bobs.

'What?' little Bobs asked, confused.

'Bow!' insisted Bibs. Not waiting for little Bobs, Bibs bowed his head long and low, in the best way a snail can.

'Greetings,' he grovelled, 'greetings, Number Twenty Three of the First Ones. Greetings Eerht Ytnewt On!'

Rielle and Pud looked from the bowing Bibs to Old, then at each other.

Little Bobs stood by, confused.

Old surprised Rielle with his response. 'No time for curtsy. Come with us to the Tower of Dreams.'

Bibs looked up, frowning. 'Uh,' he began, 'excuse me Your Great One, but I had a frightful time last time I was there.'

'No begging.' Old began to walk on ahead. 'No begging. We need little friends for the low places on the ground.' It was obvious from Old's posture that it was not a request.

Bibs looked at Rielle with a question in his eyes.

Rielle shrugged and crossed her arms. 'Don't look at *me*,' she said, smiling grimly. 'I don't want to go there either, but I have no choice!'

Bibs looked at Pud, but Pud just grinned, sneezed and nudged him so hard that Bibs fell over and landed upside down.

'Hey,' Bibs called, 'be careful! Is no so eezy getting op when you me!'

Poking his head into Bibs' shell, little Bobs grinned and poked out his tongue. 'Now it's your turn!' he cried.

'Nob fo wong,' Bibs yelled, 'nob fo wong I won bi!' With the practise that comes from age, Bibs struggled and grunted and gritted his teeth. He groaned, but soon he was the right way up again. 'Wait for me!' he called to the disappearing group.

In Old's hand, the Wand of Time still led the way. Its pale wood glowed softly as it leaned toward something unseen.

Walking quickly, Rielle whispered to Old, 'Will you tell me, now, what I asked before?'

Old looked at her with deliberate focus. 'The Wand of Time seeks her own kind; even as it is, I search for the others.'

Excitement flooded through Rielle for some reason she didn't understand.

'The wand is telling you where to find the others?' she asked eagerly.

'Perhaps,' Old replied, 'only perhaps.'

'Who is the wand leading you to, then?' Rielle was confused.

Old stopped. He peered around carefully. In the background they could hear Bibs calling for them to wait.

'When it is safe to speak the words,' Old murmured, 'I will let you know.'

'I'm here!' Bibs called loudly as he caught up. 'I have been summoned by a great one, and I am here to honour the call!'

With one thought, Rielle and Old turned and glared at him.

'Shhhhhhhh!' they both exclaimed.

CHAPTER 13

Willful James

In a soundless flash, Oobaat and the unicorn herd appeared in Wish. The unicorns stepped quietly. For many of them, Wish was strange, unfamiliar and new. Oobaat and Coraggio looked guardedly at each other.

'I believe we are in the almond orchard,' Oobaat murmured.

'Yes,' Coraggio agreed, 'this is the part they call the Valley of Possibility.'

Taking stock of their surroundings, the herd looked up. Some distance away the steeples of the Tower of Dreams emerged, their pinnacles reaching to the sky.

'This way, then,' Candela directed, and as one, they all followed her lead.

...

In Hope's chamber, Will abruptly woke. Without moving, he opened his eyes. His mind was foggy but he clearly remembered Far and Hope. Sunlight dribbled dainty sprinkles of filtered joy about the simple, neat chamber. Will gaped, enthralled; several huge pots boiled in different places, without a visible fire or flame. He raised himself onto an elbow, amazed at how much strength he had.

'Hello?' he whispered. He swung his feet to the floor. 'Is anyone here?' he asked more boldly.

He noticed he was dressed in something warm and white, knitted from soft wool. He looked around for his clothes. They were folded neatly by the bed, clean and pressed, but still full of holes. Will searched for his shoes. They weren't there. He frowned at that, annoyed, and then remembered they'd been full of holes and didn't keep out either rain or burs.

The room was empty and no one responded to Will's call. He wondered how long he had slept. He had been well looked after, that much was certain. Quickly, he changed from the nightshirt he was wearing back into his own clothes, but then wasn't sure what to do next.

Briefly, he thought of escape, but the room seemed to have no door and the windows were blocked by huge simmering pots. *Escape from what exactly? Escape from someone who gave me solace and made me well?* He realised how silly that seemed. Ashamed, he frowned at the thought. Restlessly he walked around, feeling better than he could remember. Peeking into a huge stewing pot, he recoiled at the black sticky substance within.

A flash of sunlight shimmered boldly through a window, briefly touching the back walls of the room. Will followed it with his eyes. In the darkest corner, a small door stood slightly ajar. Just as quickly, the sunlight retreated and left the corner dark once more.

A glow-worm of curiosity lit Will's mind. Fetching a candle that flickered faintly, he crept to where he'd seen the door. Darkness and shadows greeted him. He stopped, puzzled. There was only a solid wall, an old trunk and a large, old chair. Will turned away, but then turned back, willing the candle flame to show him the doorway. It still wasn't there.

He had another idea. Closing his eyes, he held out a hand. Cold air brushed his hand, showing him he'd found an opening. Will grinned in triumph. The doorway was quite low and narrow, as if it had been built for a smaller type of person. Stooping, Will wrenched the door open wide, straining to see what was on the other side. Darkness greeted him.

'Hello?' he whispered.

No one answered. Chill air blew around his face and feet. He held the candle up to the dark, but the flame spluttered and died. Placing the spent candle onto the floor, he checked over his shoulder as if someone might be watching.

Outside, the sun blazed warmly and a soft haze filled the peace of Hope's room. Books bound in hand-sewn leather lay open and closed on benches and a table. Herbs were drying on wicker pallets, their scent drifting sweetly. Reaching from floor to ceiling, the walls housed shelves filled with books and a huge array of bottles filled with liquids of many colours.

Will glanced at the bunk he had lain on. It looked so very comfortable. Peace triumphed in Hope's room and tugged at Will's restless spirit. A part of Will's mind asked for more sleep but Will challenged the urge and fought it instead.

Grabbing his hat, he turned back to the darkness of the doorway, and barefoot, he stepped through. Coloured lights flashed through his head and burst through his mind. He felt himself falling, but it didn't hurt, and then, suddenly, he was lying on grass. He lay still, winded and surprised. Birds sang and crickets chirped. A warm breeze carried a scent.

Will grunted and sat up. Pink and white blossoms drifted slowly from above, making the ground fragrant with their many spent blooms.

'What the,' Will breathed, 'what the blazes? I'm outside, somehow!'

He stood, pivoting to gain his bearings. In the near distance he could see the topmost pinnacle of a tower.

'Is that where I was?' he wondered aloud. 'But, how did I get from there to here?' He supposed he should go back. After all, Hope and Far had been very kind.

Almond trees spread as far as he could see. They had an air of secretive peace that intrigued his sensibilities. Almond nuts that were still in their shells crunched under his feet, making Will grin. He didn't know what Hope had done for him, but he felt vibrant and free!

I'll go back in a minute, he thought, but the minutes lengthened, until Will forgot all about time.

...

The herd and Oobaat moved forward without a sound. Birds sang, trees creaked and leaves whispered secrets, as the sun shone around them. Wish had never seen so many unicorns!

Coraggio stopped. 'What's that?' he whispered.

Like soldiers marching, the herd halted as if by command.

A voice floated downwind toward them. It was singing. The unicorns winced. The voice sang badly:

I have my whole life left
To find my way home from this strange place
They call it Wish, they say it's easy
But how do I get home agaaaiiinnnn?

Coraggio and Candela's eyes met and held.

'It's been a long time, my dear,' Coraggio murmured.

'Yes husband,' Candela breathed, 'but it looks like fate has chosen this moment.'

'We can avoid him if you like,' Coraggio urged. 'This is not a part of our plan.'

Candela's poise shone through her velvet eyes. 'No,' she breathed, 'fate has chosen this significant moment, so that must mean we will meet now for a purpose.'

Again, she and Coraggio held a glance.

The singing was moving closer.

Oobaat looked at Candela. 'I think you have no need to be alarmed,' he prompted. 'He sounds lost, alone and harmless.'

'Yes, good Oobaat,' Candela responded, 'he was always lost; that was the problem.'

'*I'm in Wish,*' the voice warbled, '*but how do I get out again?*'

Without another word, Candela left her herd and her husband's side. She stepped forward, dignity glowing from her like an antique truth. Her horn told her that there was no danger here.

Like silent watchers and keepers of unity, the unicorns stood stock still.

The voice hummed closely. The herd waited for its owner to appear.

Will rounded a bend in the path and began to open his mouth to sing again, when he looked up. He choked on the words beginning in his throat. White bodies stood like a wall of honour, and dozens of velvet eyes watched him, like a silent verdict. It claimed Will's breath; he turned to run.

Quietly - so quietly that it seemed he would not hear - Candela spoke.

'Willful James, we meet again.'

The herd took a united step forward.

Candela stayed one step in front.

Will knew they could outrun him should he even try to flee. His shoulders slumped and something like a sob caught in his throat. With a dread he believed he would never feel again, he turned to face them.

Candela examined him. Will's clothes were tattered and torn. Marks showed empty spaces where jewels had once sparkled from his ridiculous hat, and he had lost his shoes. He was still a handsome young man, but the years spent being a small bent shrub showed in little ways. Will's mouth was sad and his eyes dull; he looked like an old man trapped in youth.

Will could not look up.

Candela waited. The herd waited. Silence thundered around them.

Will knew they were waiting for *him*. With a sob, he fell raggedly to his knees.

'Please,' he implored, 'please believe me when I tell you I have spent forever begging you for your forgiveness!'

Candela stepped right up to the lump that he had become.

'Then ask for it now, Willful James,' she whispered. 'Ask now, for I am here.'

With a gesture that made the herd rush forward, Will grasped Candela's legs. Candela turned her head and glimpsed at the herd; they steadied in their steps and once more became a solid wall of white protection.

'Forgive me,' Will blubbered with his heart fully breaking. 'Forgive me for my cruel, stupid action. I tried to harm you - I know that now - but when I did it I was young and....'

Candela waited.

Despite himself, Will looked at her. He met her eyes. She was so beautiful that she took his breath away. Slowly he stood and removed his hat.

The herd sighed. Oobaat nodded and watched the scene unfold.

Will continued. 'Back then, in my days of youth and glory, I just saw you as a creature - an animal to slay - so that I could use your horn for its hidden powers.' He paused as his heart continued to break. 'I didn't even see your beauty then. I didn't see who you were.'

Will's breath shuddered. 'I was stupid... careless... greedy! So I... I've lived alone and trapped, and regretted each and every day.' Tears coursed down his face, leaving trails of dusty sadness on his hollow cheeks.

Before he knew what he was doing, Will put out a hand and touched Candela's graceful neck. Her skin shone like burnished silk and her coat felt like buttery velvet.

Coraggio took another step forward and Oobaat took several strides. The herd bunched their muscles just in case.

Will gazed with wonder at Candela. White light poured from her like a delicate perfume and her silken mane and tail caressed the ground. He looked at her shoulder - the one he'd shot with his cruel crossbow. With exquisite care, Will touched the spot where the wound would have been. There was not even a visible scar. Standing taller, Will looked Candela fully in the eye.

'At least I managed to do one thing right,' he breathed, 'and that was to give you my healing leaves.' He sighed. 'When I first became the shrubby bush, I thought it would be forever. I had no idea that once all the leaves were gone, I'd become human again.' He wiped the tears from his face, leaving a pathetic muddy smear.

'Perhaps that's the hardest part, for it's been a long, long reckoning, lovely unicorn. I know I still look young, but inside I'm just plain tired. Once I thought I wanted to live forever, but now I know what a burden that would be.'

Will kneeled once more before Candela and bowed his head.

'Forgive me, innocent unicorn. Forgive me for my treacherous act. I want to erase this pain of guilt from my heart, yet I know that I never can. Please forgive me. Please. Set me free to begin again.'

Candela thought carefully about Will's words. He had shot her with a dangerous arrow. She must be cautious now in what she said and did.

'You came to Wish with one desire,' she began evenly, 'and that was to steal a unicorn horn.'

Oobaat winced inwardly. If only Candela knew the wishes he heard!

Candela paused then continued. 'Of all the wishes you could have made, that was the one you chose. Wish could have granted you anything that your heart desired, but you shot me, aiming for my heart. Luck let my shoulder take the wound, but your desire was to steal a power that was not yours. However, Willful James,' Candela breathed, 'even if the power could have passed to you, you would never have known how to use it. It would all have been for nothing and a terrible waste.' She lowered her head and allowed her words to sink in. 'Only unicorns can wield their power, just as you have power of your own.'

Will's head jolted up. 'I have power of my own?'

'Yes,' Candela countered, 'but it's not what you think, Willful James.' She peered watchfully at him. 'Be careful now. Make wise choices. Do not be weak, selfish, or a coward.' Candela found no other words to give him. He would have to find his own way now. A shadow crossed her heart, but she kept it from her face.

'Thank you,' Will whispered, 'thank you for giving me pardon. I won't forget it, and I promise I won't betray you again.' He looked openly at her, meeting her gaze. Her velvet eyes hid nothing and her beauty and greatness gave him grace.

'Keep that promise, Willful James,' Candela urged. 'Hold it, and remember you have made it, for now you have been twice blessed; and blessings are precious and given in trust.'

Will stood up.

The herd faced him like an impenetrable truth.

'I never knew there were so many of you,' Will murmured to their knowing faces.

Oobaat walked over to Will.

Will gaped at Oobaat, surprised. 'I didn't notice you before,' he stammered. 'Do you lead the unicorn herd?'

Oobaat chuckled without humour. 'Lead them?' he repeated. 'No… nobody leads the mighty unicorns. We walk together at times.'

Will blushed and nodded as if he had been chastised. 'You remind me of someone,' he muttered to Oobaat, 'but I can't think who it is.'

Oobaat smiled; it was a kind smile. He very much wanted things to go well for the young man, but something cast gloom on his heart.

'Remember Will,' Oobaat cautioned, 'blessings are precious and given in trust. Those who break promises to others, and themselves, risk losing grace, and relinquish their power. A blessing is precious, and if you scorn it, there is always a price of some kind to pay.' He looked closely at Will, making him blanch. 'Do you understand?'

Will glanced at Candela. She watched him piercingly.

He gazed around at the rest of the herd. They tossed their heads and some pawed the ground.

'Yes,' Will whispered, humbled, 'yes, I truly understand.' And then, because he couldn't take it anymore, because their truth was too hard to bear, Will turned at last, and ran.

'Thank you!' he called over his shoulder. 'Thank you!'

Will ran toward the tower, as fast as his bare feet would let him. He wanted nothing more than to hide in Hope's room and to go back to sleep for a long, long blissful time.

CHAPTER 14

Are we alike or are we not
So let us meet where time forgot

The Wand of Time led Old on, pulsing at the air like a beacon on a sallow night of mist. Old began to trot and Pud followed promptly, checking that his mistress was by his side. Rielle wasn't sure why they needed to run but she trusted Old. She began to jog. Bibs and little Bobs glanced briefly at each other, and then they too picked up speed. The group passed through strange, alien gullies where the grass grew well except for small patches of odd discoloured ground.

'Do not step on bare patches,' Old pointed a warning, as he continued to run.

The breeze, which had whispered quietly around them, was beginning to lash at leaves on trees. Boughs and branches were also becoming stretched and beaten, as if by fury. Soon, running became a test of patience as the wind beat against them, pushing them back.

Rielle began to struggle. However, the Wand of Time kept tugging Old forward, so all they could do was follow. They ran through a sullen gully where trees had the mark of doubt, and no bird or animal, of any kind, greeted them with a call or cry. The wind raged in screaming torment. Rielle wondered if they would ever leave this cheerless place. At last the gully lurched uphill and took them onto high, brighter ground. Old stopped. The Wand of Time strained so strongly that he held it back with both hands.

'Hush!' He seemed to barely whisper the command, but command it was. Somehow Rielle heard Old speak above the roar of the wind. She wondered whether he was hushing the wand, or if the words were meant for the rest of them.

Old was watching something that the others couldn't see. Urgently, the wand lurched forward as if it could fly away on its own. Old gasped and struggled, keeping it in check with all the strength in his powerful arms. He grasped for the golden cloth and covered the wand from top to bottom. Immediately, the wand became a mellow stick in his hand.

Rielle went to speak, but as if reading her mind, Old held a finger up to bid her quiet. Without a word, he turned and pointed. Instantly, Pud's hackles rose and he barely suppressed a growl. Rielle had seen Pud like that only once before and the memory flooded her with shivers of dread like no other. Fearfully she looked to where Old pointed. Rielle covered her mouth to stop her gasp.

In the deep of a gully, a dark-draped figure strode to and fro, a walking wand held in its hand. The wand glowed red at its centre.

Rielle caught Old's eye. He merely nodded.

Pud stood frozen, his mouth poised in a grim, teeth-bared growl with his back tight and tail poised. It was Bibs, though, that surprised them all; he had curled into a trembling ball. Seeing his cousin like that, little Bobs began to cry.

'Hush!' Old gestured, not unkindly, before hunkering down to whisper something to Bibs. The others looked on curiously, but whatever Old said, it worked. Bibs uncurled and crept forward. They all huddled together then, sheltering behind a pocket of trees as winds raged and stormed around them like crazed, howling spectres.

The figure in the distance raised his walking wand, mouthing words the group could not hear. The wind flailed and roared at his feet as he gestured and tugged at its unwilling ends.

Then, unexpectedly, the winds stopped. In the shock of silence, Rielle looked away. Her eyes locked with Pud and then with Old. No one moved. The stillness threatened them as much as the noise. When Rielle looked back again, the dark figure was gone.

Old turned from the group with a gleam in his eye.

'Trouble,' he hissed through grim, clenched lips, 'trouble has come at last!'

Pud snarled low in his throat. Rielle feared he was ready to leap. Instead, he stepped forward stiffly and stood closer to her. Placing a paw onto her shoe, Pud nudged her before pushing his muzzle into her hand. Rielle held him close and then glanced at the snails. They were hidden inside their shells.

The star-scar on Rielle's forehead began to burn

painfully hot. Rielle knew what that meant. The small hairs stood up on her neck. Her heart thumped with sick new fear. She turned to look behind her.

Like a raw omen, Pud strangled a growl.

A dark presence stood on the hilltop beside them, blocking all means of escape. The group froze.

'So,' the Sorcerer of Great Contempt sneered, 'Number Twenty Three, *Eerht ytnewt On*, what brings you out from wherever you've been hiding?'

Old delayed before answering. With a look about him that seemed ready to leap, he stoically faced the sorcerer.

'Trouble,' he growled.

'Hmm, trouble, trouble,' scoffed the sorcerer, 'let me see, this er... trouble... *that wouldn't be me?*' Through fierce black lips he scornfully grinned.

In Rielle's eyes, Old seemed to grow beyond his few feet. With a quick movement that defied the eye, Old unravelled the golden cloth and held the Wand of Time up high.

'Do not challenge, Number Seven, *Neves On!* Do not challenge, for I have here the Wand of Time!'

The sorcerer roared with grim elation. 'Do not challenge? Fool,' he cried, 'do you know what it is I have here?' With a wild gesture he raised his own walking wand.

In that moment, Rielle knew that something had changed unpromisingly.

The sorcerer held up the staff he wielded. It was made of pure white wood and yet it glowed at its centre, a molten red. Old gave a shout that struck new terror into the hearts of his little group. They sensed his confusion.

'Not possible!' Old rasped. 'Not possible for you to hold this power!'

Old turned to the group. 'Run,' he bellowed for the second time that day. 'Run! Run like never before!'

Rielle hesitated but it was too late. Old and the sorcerer had vanished.

'Old!' she screamed with a sob in her throat. 'Old! Are you alright?' A roar of silence followed.

Boldly, startling Rielle, Bibs leapt up. 'This way!' Bibs surprised her. 'This way, all of you, follow me!'

Rielle hesitated, waiting to see if Old would reappear. Her foot nudged something. She looked down. On the ground were Old's cake tin and the golden cloth. Quickly she scooped them up. Scrunching the cloth into a tight ball she jammed it inside the golden cake tin. Then, clutching the cake tin tightly, she turned to Bibs.

'Follow me,' bawled Bibs, 'he said run, so run!'

Anxious for Old, Rielle reluctantly followed Pud and the snails.

Bibs led them across silent rock passes and crevices hidden beneath giant trees. He took them under boulders that hung cleverly over cliffs, and through fern-ridden places that no one else knew was there.

As she went, Rielle thought of Old's soft doeskin hands, his big brown eyes and his childlike concern. She thought of his delicious cake and the Wand of Time, and she thought of his sweet upturned smile.

Did she push him to leave the cave - the place where he'd been safe for so long? Had the choice to leave been his? What would happen to him now? Was Number Twenty Three of the

First Ones any match for the Sorcerer of Great Contempt? Would they ever see Old again?

Even as she ran, Rielle searched for the safe, strong back of her mysterious new friend. Pud looked up at his mistress. Sensing her bewilderment and loss, he gently took her hand in his mouth as they escaped through places that only a snail would know.

'Thank you Pud,' Rielle breathed, 'you are my best of all friends.' Pud's encouragement lent new wings to her feet. 'We have to find help,' she called out to the others. 'There must be some way to get Old back!'

Bibs and little Bobs slid with flattened antennae and their heads pushed forward like the guardians they were. Pud ran, as he always did, with ease, speed and a sense of purpose. Rielle wasn't sure they'd heard her. She knew they would have to go back to find Old, but for now they needed to reach safety.

Rounding a bend, Rielle's heart lifted. Miraculously, they were in the almond orchard, in the Valley of Possibility. *Clever Bibs!* Rielle remembered the orchard from the last time she'd been in Wish; she and Pud been running away that time too, but in the opposite direction.

She looked up. The tower was still far away. The almond orchard was vast. 'I never thought, Pud,' Rielle wheezed, 'that I'd be happy to see this place again.'

In some places the orchard was so dense that it kept them dodging and diving. Ducking, Rielle had some near misses with low hanging branches. At times she would drop her head and close her eyes in case branches or leaves would poke her in the face.

Rielle… Rielle… Rielle!

Rielle slowed and looked back. The voice was calling her again!

'Look out!' Rielle heard someone cry, and then, before she knew it, she was lying flat on the ground. She groaned. Something had hit her hard and fast. Pud barked loudly, then ran to Rielle's side and licked her face.

Rielle sat up. A young man was sitting on the grass nearby, looking at her crossly and rubbing his head.

'What in blazes were *you* doing?' the young man bellowed, a look of disgust on his face.

Rielle was shocked. It wasn't her fault they'd collided!

'What the hooley dooley were *you* doing?' she bellowed back.

'You crashed into me!' he yelled.

Rielle gasped, enraged. 'You crashed into *me!*' she roared.

They glared at each other with furious faces.

Bibs and little Bobs had disappeared from sight but Pud stood anxiously by his mistress.

Rielle felt the new bump on her head. 'You might be decent enough to ask how I am.' She frowned, sizing up the young man in his ragged clothes.

'You look fine to me,' he spat.

Rielle stood up and so did Will.

'I'd ask how you are,' Rielle rounded on Will, 'but judging by your big mouth, you seem just fine!'

Bibs and little Bobs reappeared. 'Are you alright?' Bibs asked Rielle.

'Thank you Bibs, I'm alright,' Rielle retorted. 'Let's get away from here and keep going.' She glanced scornfully at the stranger. He had picked up his hat and put it back on his head. He was fidgeting as if he wanted to say something but wasn't sure how.

'Come on,' Rielle said to Pud and the snails, 'let's go. We have to find Hope if we can, and tell him what's happened.'

'Wait,' Will cut in, 'did you say Hope?'

'What's it to you?' Rielle spat, as she started to walk away.

'I… well, I know Hope… a little,' Will answered. 'I know where he is… at least some of the time.'

Rielle stopped. 'What are you saying?' she asked.

'Let me show you where Hope is,' Will stammered. 'It's, well, the least that I can do.'

'Can you show us fast?' Rielle asked, excited. 'We need to find him as soon as we can!'

Again Will looked as if he wanted to say something, but instead, his eyes lit up, and beginning to run, he called, 'Follow me!'

CHAPTER 15

A thousand years or moments ago

Splashing colour over Wish, the sun began seeking an end to another long day. Flickers of orange toffee speckled the almond trees, turning pink and white flowers into orange and gold.

Standing tall and holding the Wand of Faith as if it were an offering, Hope waited. Far and Flightlord stood solemnly by, unsure what would happen next. From the moment Hope had brought out the wand, he had continued to hold it like an offering, as if that in itself was somehow important.

They had left Will to his sleeping, and gone out into the orchard.

Hope waited.

As the sun spent its last moments in goodbye, so did the wand's centre spring to life. It began to glow, and then its voice leapt in song:

With the moon that comes to greet us
And the sun that leaves each day
Reach out, reach out
With a summons and a prayer!

Suddenly, the Wand of Faith wasn't singing alone! A similar voice joined in the melting melody. The two voices sang:

Spirit, Fire, Air, Earth and Water
Moon, Stars, Sun and Sky
The Truth of Time we have been seeking
Destiny we are now meeting

With power earned
Of truth, of love
Justice, honour
Duty strong

With The Wand of Faith
With The Staff of Life
Forward, together
All tasks are not done

This day has come
A battle to be had, a battle to be won
Unicorn and First Ones
All seeing, all strong

Beyond the surface
Beyond the surface
Unicorn and First Ones
So shall it be done!

The sun snapped shut. Night had arrived. The orchard

was completely still. Then, the darkness began to move and sway. From the shifting shadows, Oobaat stepped forward. He greeted Hope.

'Salutations Enin On, Number Nine of the First Ones!'

Hope replied calmly, as if they met most days. In truth they had not encountered one another for some thousand years or more.

'Greetings Eno On, Number One of the First Ones.'

The herd stood back.

Oobaat and Hope faced each other. The Wand of Faith and the Staff of Life glowed brightly.

'So,' Hope said, studying Oobaat. 'So, this time you have borrowed human shape?'

Grimly, Oobaat laughed. 'Yes,' he replied, 'unicorns have spoken, and they will have their way.'

The First Ones chuckled as if sharing an old private joke. Hope nodded his understanding. They looked fondly at each other, with eyes that spoke of their brotherhood.

The herd moved forward as if on cue.

Coraggio explained. 'Greetings, Enin On. It is true. The herd needed help and this was the best way we knew.'

Candela didn't bother with formalities. She beamed joyfully as she greeted the First One. 'Enin On,' she called softly, 'so much time has passed. How wonderful to meet again.'

With deepest respect for his beloved friend, Hope bowed formally.

'Dear Candela,' he breathed, 'how long has it been?'

'More than a thousand years,' she replied, 'yet to see

you again warms my heart so gladly, it feels like it was just weeks ago.' They beamed happily at each other with the understanding of those who cherish long friendships.

A hush flooded the orchard. The light from the wands had gone out. There was no moon as yet, and the darkness was dense.

'Come,' Hope whispered, 'we must enter the tower.' With one thought, he and Oobaat tapped their walking wands to the ground. Instantly, they were all transported inside the tower.

As usual, the Tower of Dreams issued peace. Muted warm light flowed from some unknown source buried within its unfathomably high walls.

Hope strode up and down as if he wasn't sure where to begin. At last he stopped pacing and looked fully at the herd.

'What,' he exclaimed, shocked, 'so many of you? Can it be? Can it be this is the *entire* Lilifel?'

The herd did not respond. They watched him calmly.

Dismay rode in Hope's face and voice. 'You have *all* come to Wish?' He hesitated in disbelief. 'Is it wise, my friends? Is it wise to do such a thing?' He searched their faces for understanding, and then continued with new urgency. 'Do you not fear for the Ritual of Return?'

Oobaat stepped forward. 'Enin On,' he proclaimed, 'we have terrible news. There is a reason for this strange journey.'

Hope didn't wait for Oobaat to explain. He stood tall, his eyes blazing.

'It's *him*, isn't it? I have sensed as much! Nothing else

could be so important as to risk the entire Lilifel in this dangerous place!' Hope held up his hand as Oobaat went to speak. 'I sensed a stirring when the butterfly returned to me without the girl and the dog.'

Benny gasped. 'Was it perhaps a ball of wind that plunged the butterfly through the river and on to the other side?'

Hope paused and shut his eyes. He held the Wand of Faith in one hand and smoothed its dark brown wood with the other. The wand hummed a happy sound. Oobaat and the unicorns waited.

'Indeed,' Hope answered at last, as if privately grieving, 'indeed it was.' He gave Benny a knowing look then continued to address the meeting.

'I would have chosen this reunion to take place in happy times.' Hope sighed and placed a brotherly hand on Oobaat's shoulder. 'I have not looked upon the Wand of Faith or heard her voice for so long that I had forgotten her peace and joy.' He gazed around. 'My place has been here, in the Tower of Dreams, performing my duties for any that need me, and that includes human-kind. It's been so long that I have almost forgotten other times.'

He smiled wistfully. 'Here, I am known as Hope, and that has been enough for me.' He looked at Oobaat kindly. 'Tell me brother,' he asked, 'tell me, wasn't it hard to leave your duties and your beloved pond because of him... the undeserving one?'

Oobaat nodded in cheerless agreement. 'We should try to find Eerht ytnewt On,' he ventured, cautiously.

Hope sighed. 'Yes, that is, if Number Twenty Three

can be found,' he replied, sagely.

The unicorns shifted restlessly.

Brimming with urgency, Benny interrupted. 'Number Seven of The First Ones, Neves On, or, as he's called in Wish, the Sorcerer of Great Contempt... he rules the wind. That's why your butterfly left Rielle and Pud.'

Hope pulled back from speaking with Oobaat. 'Number Seven governs the wind? How do you know this?' he barked.

'I saw it.' Benny then told Hope what he had seen.

Far flew onto Hope's shoulder. She waited for Benny to finish.

'It's true,' she whispered to the gathering. 'That is exactly what happened to me.'

The unicorns stepped closer to Hope and Oobaat. They looked silently at the First Ones with one thought on their minds. It was Coraggio, however, who whispered into the corners of the hall.

'Do you realise what this means?'

Oobaat and Hope looked at each other. In one voice, they stammered the unthinkable. 'There is only one way Number Seven could govern the wind,' they gasped. 'If it is possible he has her in his possession, he could do this only if he wields the *Staff of the Unimaginable!*'

Flightlord had been standing apart from the others. Silently, he joined them. 'Not the Staff of the Unimaginable?' he hissed. 'Do we have proof? Is there no other way he could rule the wind?'

'None,' Candela announced serenely but with hidden ire, 'none. He has the most powerful wand of all; the white wand that was made for unicorns.'

'If you will pardon me, then,' Flightlord exclaimed, 'I must give this news to my people! We live by the wind. They need to know!'

Flightlord waited for no one. The world of dragon was ruled by no other; they lived by their laws alone. As quickly as he made his announcement, Flightlord was gone.

Far was still perched on Hope's shoulder. In a voice that could barely be heard, she asked, 'Why me? Why did the sorcerer bring me back to Wish in such a way? What difference could that possibly make? I mean, I'm not important or anything. I was on a mission to help Rielle find her dream.' She paused, confused. 'I wasn't doing anything that would matter to him.'

'Indeed,' Coraggio agreed, 'but think, think! We must all think! Why bring you back? He knows you are Hope's butterfly, so what could it mean?'

'It must have something to do with Rielle!' Benny exclaimed. 'After all, if he wanted to destroy the butterfly that would have been easy, so he isn't angry with Far.' Benny faced the meeting. 'He stole Far... don't you see? Far was meant to be with Rielle. It must be something to do with Rielle.'

Candela tossed her head and trilled. 'Rielle can be headstrong and impatient at times.' She paused and smiled. 'But she is a good girl, kind and wise beyond her years.' Candela's eyes flashed an idea. 'It seems to me, when I put two and two together, that if Rielle lost something that wasn't hers.... '

Grasping the thought, Benny finished her sentence in a rush. 'She would come to Wish to let Hope know!'

Candela nodded, and tossed her mane.

'So,' Far puzzled, 'why would the sorcerer want Rielle back in Wish? She isn't powerful or anything. How would she make a difference to him?'

'She wouldn't,' exclaimed Oobaat, 'he doesn't want Rielle.' He turned slowly and all eyes followed. He was staring hard at Benny.

The entire herd trilled aloud, shifting tensely.

Oobaat put the thought to words. 'Ah, it makes sense now, does it not? Number Seven knows that unicorns won't come willingly to Wish, so, knowing that Benny watches over the human girl, it was vital to draw her back here somehow.'

'So this isn't about Rielle.' Coraggio stepped forward as he looked at his son. 'It's a unicorn he wants. He wants to kill a unicorn and break the Ritual of Return.' He turned to Far. 'If Benny knew that Rielle had returned to Wish and that she was in danger, then of course he would have followed her here. The Sorcerer of Great Contempt used you as bait, little butterfly. He used *you* to bring Rielle to Wish and then he was going to use *her* to draw Benny back here as well.'

Coraggio glowered. 'I fear that Rielle would never have made it to tell Hope how she had lost you, Far. In order to capture Benny, the sorcerer would have held Rielle as a hostage.' He grimaced, still looking at Far. 'It surprises me he let you return to Hope. It strikes me as odd that he let you go free once you'd returned.'

'Why do you say that?' Far whispered, shaken.

'Because,' Coraggio continued, 'your return meant that Hope was forewarned and that would be the last thing Neves On would want!'

Far flapped her wings. 'I was hurt,' she cried, 'and I had to rest for a while in a tree. It was Flightlord who brought me back to the tower. Maybe, if he hadn't come along when he did, I would never have made it on my own.' Far shuddered and crawled under Hope's collar to hide.

'There, there, you're safe now,' Hope murmured.

'Rielle is in great danger,' Benny interrupted. 'We must warn her and let her know to stay away from Wish!'

A hush settled on the hall.

Finally, Candela spoke. 'It is as we suspected, then.' She faced the assembly.

'Long, long ago when Number Seven of the First Ones first fell from grace, *the very first time*, it was in the days when we all still lived in the forest together. It was then that we, the unicorn herd and all of the First Ones - his own kin - banished him here to Wish for his evil deeds.' Candela sighed with reminiscing.

'As we all know, Wish is an ever-changing place that comes from the minds of humans. However, it was hoped that with Number One to guard the wishing gate, and with Number Nine to watch the tower, that Number Seven would come to his senses over the aeons of time.' She shook her head. Her mane swayed like corn in spring-blown fields.

Benny was impatient to find Rielle and to tell her to

stay away, but Candela held her audience captive.

Her eyes flashing, Candela continued. 'Here in Wish, there were no wands to help the sorcerer, and his power was insignificant, unimportant. Time went by. We hoped that if he stayed here long enough, he might learn other ways.' She looked meaningfully at Coraggio.

'It was when I came here alone all those years ago - the only unicorn to brave Wish - that trouble began once again. I came to ask Hope for a name for my foal and after I had done so, on my way home, Neves On tried to capture me, and in so doing, a human pierced my shoulder with an arrow. I escaped, of course, and the story is well known, yet we still hoped he might change his ways.' She stopped as if the memories broke her heart.

Coraggio took over. 'That is when a boy, a foolish human, helped the sorcerer, and was tricked. But, foolish or not, the human had a heart and managed to undo the evil act.'

Far couldn't help herself; she rushed out from under Hope's collar. 'You knew that the human was tricked?'

Coraggio turned to her as if her interruption was a puzzle.

'Yes,' he replied, 'yes, we've always known.'

Far turned to Hope. 'You see,' she whispered, 'it seems Flightlord was right. I could tell that Will wasn't all bad.' Hope smiled kindly at the butterfly but held up a finger to bid her hush. *That would be good news*, Hope thought, *however I think the hard part might be to convince Will.*

Everyone was looking at Far. Hastily she hid back inside Hope's collar.

Coraggio was puzzled. *Did Far know Will?* He wondered how she knew him. He didn't get a chance to ask. At that moment Oobaat broke the silence.

'Somehow,' Oobaat began with a pondering tone, 'somehow, the sorcerer has stolen the Staff of the Unimaginable and this is grave news.'

It was Hope's turn to confront the herd. He raised an eyebrow in query.

'How,' he began slowly, 'how is it possible for Neves On to have stolen the unicorn wand? Surely, the moment it was lost, you would have felt it in your hearts?' He waited patiently.

Candela nodded. 'Yes indeed, we did, Enin On.' She sighed deeply. 'He was sneakier and much bolder than even we thought he could be. We must be honest with you; we do not know how he stole the Staff of the Unimaginable. Perhaps we assumed wrongly that not even he would try such a thing. Our wand should have been safe where she was. We guarded her vigilantly, this I know. To my great shame I cannot answer.'

Oobaat cleared his throat. 'It's partly my fault. I, too, take part in guarding the unicorn wand. I fear that my duties as gatekeeper took my mind from the task at times. I never thought even *he* would dare such a sacrilege.'

Coraggio stepped forward. 'Fault is not important now,' he admonished, looking from Oobaat to Hope. 'It has happened, and we must move on. We all felt this trouble would come some day.' He turned to the herd. 'Whether Neves On wields our wand or not, I have felt he was ready to cause trouble again soon, in one way or another. Do not fret. With evil there is always work to do.'

Candela looked sadly at the gathering. 'Yes, but it makes everything much trickier, does it not? It means that the other wands will need to work harder than they ever have.'

Her eyes velvet pools, Candela paused. Her voice cracked on the next words. 'The Staff of the Unimaginable, *our wand*, was made for goodness and joy. How is she coping with his dark ways?'

The gathering stood with heads bowed for the missing wand.

Coraggio whispered at last. 'We will get our Staff back,' he promised. 'One day… one day we will reach her and bring her home.' He cleared his throat, all softness gone from his face. 'So, we agree on the reason Neves On wants to draw Benny back to Wish.'

The gathering became weighty. The herd and First Ones nodded.

'If the sorcerer kills a unicorn,' Coraggio persisted, 'he can, for a short time, break the Ritual of Return. All he needs is moments.' He looked at the gathering with eyes converted to pin pricks. 'If that happens, he could escape, at last, from Wish.'

'I thought it was impossible to kill a unicorn,' Far squeaked, from under Hope's collar.

The herd murmured.

'A unicorn *can* be caught outside of the forest, little Far,' Hope replied, 'and in that moment, there is a rift, a tear, in the Ritual of Return.'

Far cried out in horror.

'But,' Hope went on, 'if the herd reaches the unicorn

quickly, they can repair the Ritual of Return.'

Far flew timidly out of hiding to sit on Hope's shoulder.

'So,' she began, 'because unicorns banished the sorcerer to Wish, must they keep watch that he doesn't escape?'

Hope nodded.

'So,' Far went on more boldly, 'if the sorcerer can kill a unicorn, must the herd focus on the Ritual of Return to heal the unicorn and make it live again?'

Hope nodded.

'So,' Far continued, 'while they focus on doing that, he gains precious moments to escape. Am I right? Is that how it goes?'

Hope nodded.

Far took a deep breath. 'So,' she called loudly, forgetting herself, 'isn't it dangerous for the whole herd to be here? What if he tries to hurt more than one? Especially now he has the unicorn wand? Is that possible? Could he do that?'

Hope held up his hand to stop the butterfly's barrage of questions.

'Yes,' Coraggio replied for him, 'the whole herd being in Wish is very risky, but on the other hand, when the entire herd stay together, the Ritual of Return is almost impossible to break. We are bound like a solid wall.'

'His escape would create havoc in the outside world,' Oobaat breathed. 'With the Staff of the Unimaginable in his keeping, there is no telling what his madness would achieve.'

Hope faced the unicorn herd. 'What should we do now?' he asked.

Candela and Coraggio exchanged a glance. Coraggio stepped forward.

'When we learned that the sorcerer could rule the wind, we called the Oath of Spirit, Fire, Air, Earth and Water, and brought Oobaat back in man-shape. Together, with all of our powers combined, and only then with no holding back, will we have a chance to put an end to this!'

The gathering fell into thought.

Splintering the silence that gripped the hall, Benny stomped a hoof and tossed his curly mane.

'How do we keep Rielle away from Wish?' he trilled.

CHAPTER 16

When wizards meet

Old coasted through a dark void of mist. Frosty tendrils of fog grasped and prodded at him with slimy indifference. Old tried to sense for signs of life. Standing tall with his head held high, he poised the Wand of Time in front of him, as if ready to strike or block. The Wand of Time glowed in tune with his every thought. Pivoting on the balls of his three-toed feet, Old strained to see through the gloom. The mist offered no sound.

With hardly visible shifts, the mists began to change. Grimacing, Old sniffed the air then wrenched his eye-patch down so he could see with both eyes. A breeze flickered. He tensed. Soon the breeze became brisk slaps of wind that struck at his body and face. The currents became faster and faster, until a whirlwind spun around him.

Old waited, unmoving, with the Wand of Time held ready.

The first attack came from behind, of course, but he countered it with one swift, skilful block. Honey-coloured and white wand met. The boom of their contact cracked the silence as the whirlwind raged in fury. Old stood, right foot forward and left foot back, patience written on the blank slate of his face.

The whirlwind spent itself and died. Silence flooded the greasy mists and then the fog parted, like dull grey blankets.

Taller, much taller and almost majestic, except for his obvious corruption, the Sorcerer of Great Contempt faced Old, holding the white wand high. The First Ones cautiously circled each other in a perfect balance of opposites.

'You are short and out of practise,' the sorcerer hissed.

Old chuckled soberly. 'You are tall and cumbersome. You fight like a coward, a thief, with a wand not yours,' he quipped.

Grinning darkly through cruel, dull lips, the sorcerer grasped the white wand tightly. 'This pretty toy has no choice,' he sneered. 'While I have it in my keeping, no one can take it from me!'

Old stopped circling. He faced the villain before him. 'The wand you hold belongs to unicorns.' Old held his ground. 'Why make trouble? Much time has passed. Why make trouble once again?'

The Sorcerer of Great Contempt pointed the Staff of the Unimaginable skyward and screeched a command. Hordes of small beastly creatures swooped with razor teeth and talons towards Old.

Breathing words to his own wand, Old became a gigantic lion. With fierce teeth and jaws, the lion leapt to swallow the flying creatures, whole. Old sprang back to his feet once again. Caution etched his face. The Wand of Time united with his heartbeat.

Number Twenty Three and Number Seven of the First Ones continued to circle each other. Peril tainted the air.

'You were never important,' the sorcerer mocked spitefully. 'You are only number twenty three after all, and I am number seven.' He paused, dangerously.

Rolling his livid eyes, he went on. 'I should have been number one; we all know that! But no, traitors one and all, you chose that slow-witted dimwit, Oobaat, to be Number One of the First Ones; he with his ponderous ways!' He grinned fiercely, delighted with a private joke. 'You picked a fool, and because of him,' he paused, sneering, 'I managed to steal the unicorn wand!' He laughed aloud. 'Now it is mine forever, *brother!*'

Old narrowed his eyes into tiny slits. 'Number One of the First Ones is humble,' he rebuked. 'You are trouble. That is all.' He shifted the Wand of Time subtly in his hands. 'You steal from unicorns. Who else does that?'

Lightning slashed above Old's head, but Old transformed yet again, this time into a puddle of water, and the lightning fizzled. Old jumped to his feet. With a quiet grin he faced the sorcerer, embracing the challenge despite the danger.

'You know you cannot win,' the sorcerer spat. 'I have the Staff of the Unimaginable, you blundering fool. How can you possibly win?' He sneered. 'I've already broken your pathetic little bridge! You've seen how the wind plays to me. Do you think you have a chance, Number Twenty Three?' He sniggered; a short, harsh sound. 'You with your humble wand, a modest tool for an ordinary First One, low down in the pecking order of power!' With the Staff of the Unimaginable held high, the sorcerer swooped to crack Old's skull.

Old stood, tranquil and still as if there were no need to fight this most dangerous and dominant First One who was rushing toward him wielding the most commanding wand. Old stood, his face blank, his eyes fixed as if seeing something else. He stood as if everything had stopped, but in his hands the Wand of Time glowed at her core. Old breathed words to her:

I hold the Wand of Time
I hold the Wand of Time
Things I make, they cannot break
I hold the Wand of Time.

Then, gently, Old tapped the wand.
The Wand of Time's voice soared. She sang:

Truth of Time we have been seeking
Destiny we are meeting!

Although the Staff of the Unimaginable was clutched powerfully in the sorcerer's hands, hearing the verse sung by a sister wand tugged at a fading certainty. Pinpricks of memory reminded the white wand who she really was. She swerved, screaming, as if her heart were breaking.

She was made by unicorns, the mighty unicorns who lived by justice and truth and who loved her well.

The Staff of the Unimaginable leapt and twisted from the sorcerer's hands to land far from Old. She lay unmoving.

The sorcerer shrieked, enraged. Disbelief at being so easily thwarted, he glared at Old. 'You will pay for this, you nobody,' he hissed, scooping the Staff of the Unimaginable from the ground. Once more he clenched her in his unyielding fist. The white wand glowed red at her centre, but in a small voice that could no longer sing, she softly wept.

In his heart, Old bled for the captive wand. He almost allowed anger to rob him of his calm but he controlled the urge, knowing it would be his undoing in the menace of the moment. He faced the sorcerer knowing that now he must escape or surely die. Number Seven of the First Ones did not take defeat well. History had shown this in many unfortunate ways.

With renewed stealth the sorcerer faced Old. 'That little trick will only work once,' he whispered, 'I warn you.'

Number Seven and Number Twenty Three circled one another. The sorcerer knew not to underestimate his opponent now, despite holding the greater wand.

The ground below Old opened and molten soil poured forth to engulf him, but Old transformed himself into a swallow and rose above it to fly away.

The ground closed, but a bird of prey chased him, so Old plummeted to earth to become a stone. The bird of prey screeched to a stop and sat on the stone, its talons digging into it without mercy. The stone became the jaws of a tiger and the bird of prey screamed and soared out of reach just in time to turn into a rush of enormous hailstones, but the tiger became fire and the hail melted in mid-fall.

A river roared to douse the fire, but the fire became an ocean, and the ocean engulfed the river and made its waters a slave. Waves crashed and fought one another, but Old became a mountain and the waves were brought to a futile end as they hit hard against the mountain's walls.

Undefeated, the river rose to become a comet, descending with blinding speed toward the mountain. The mountain dissolved to become ocean once more, and the comet plunged deep into the ocean, breaking into a million useless pieces.

As themselves once again, the First Ones faced each other.

'I will vanquish,' the sorcerer grimaced, 'and then I will find and steal your gold.' He smiled at the shift in Old's eyes. 'I will steal all the gold from your mountain caves, and make it mine.'

'Not possible,' Old whispered. 'It is hidden from prying eyes.'

'Not from mine,' the sorcerer scorned. 'I found the bridge, your bridge; I will find your caves.' He laughed. 'I will kill a unicorn and break the Ritual of Return, and then, I will take your gold.'

'Unicorns cannot be killed,' Old breathed, 'only stopped until they rise again.'

'That's where you are wrong,' the sorcerer whispered. 'I will find a way to **get** a unicorn. I nearly succeeded once before.' He grinned through blackened teeth. 'I find *humans* can be handy for these things.'

'Trouble can only kill itself in the end!' Old cried, and with a swift, unexpected rush, he managed by wonderful luck to knock the Staff of the Unimaginable from Neves On's hands.

In the split second of confusion that followed, Old brought flames up to bar the way. Hitting the ground with the Wand of Time, he vanished in a rush of light. The sorcerer called to the white wand, but it was too late; Old was gone.

Old landed in a warm place, gently lit, where voices murmured urgently.

'Do I interrupt?' Old asked.

Dozens of unicorn eyes, plus Hope, Oobaat and Far, turned in unison at his quiet, gentle voice.

'Ah… Number Twenty Three,' Oobaat breathed with a sigh of relief, 'somehow I knew you'd find us… and just in time!'

CHAPTER 17

Stars will show the way

'Hurry,' Will called, 'the sun is setting. Dark is coming, and the tower is still far away!'

Rielle, Pud and the snails eyed the growing shadows as they ran. Will was right. It wouldn't do to be caught out in Wish at night, not even in the almond orchard with the tower's pinnacles in their sight. They would be safe inside the tower. They ran on.

'Look! We're getting close!' Rielle called.

'Not close enough,' Will urged.

Like a dark invader of their calm and with no warning, the night suddenly clamped them in the black curtain of its arms. Rielle bumped into Will who had abruptly stopped.

'Sorry… ' she whispered, as if the darkness would chastise her for speaking too loudly.

Pud nudged Rielle and stayed snug by her side. Not because he was frightened but in case she was.

'What do we do now, I wonder?' Bibs muttered.

'We curl up in our shells and go to sleep,' little Bobs grumbled, exhausted and dismayed by this difficult adventure.

'No,' Bibs replied, 'no, I don't think it's as easy as that, little Bobs. Not here in Wish, anyway.' He paused. 'At least, it wasn't that simple last time I was here.'

'Well, if this place is so spooky and scary, I don't know why you brought me here,' little Bobs whispered.

Ashamed, Bibs hung his head. 'I'm truly sorry, young cousin,' he replied, 'it's all been a big mistake. I hope you'll believe me and forgive me, some day.'

'There's not even a moon,' Rielle cut in. 'At least with some moonlight we could see each other.'

'Hush,' Will interrupted, 'hush, let me think.' He shivered, even though the night was warm. 'We can't see anything in this confounded darkness, so we can't attempt to reach the tower.'

'Couldn't we keep going in the direction we think we should go?' Rielle asked. 'I don't think I fancy staying out here tonight.'

'No,' Will replied, 'no. If we keep on going, even if we only walk, we risk becoming completely lost, and I don't fancy that.' He kicked the ground. 'Darn,' he muttered, 'I don't want to scare anyone, but the last time I slept outside in the dark in Wish, it didn't do me any good.' A memory of nightmares flashed through Will's thoughts. He pushed them away.

'Look', little Bobs called out urgently, 'up there, up there, look, look!'

They all looked up.

'What is it?' Rielle breathed, amazed.

Pud yipped and Bibs held his breath.

'Star trails,' Will answered. 'Star trails!'

'But how is it happening?' Bibs asked.

'I'm not sure,' Will replied, 'but I think it has something to do with Wish.'

'It must be,' Rielle exclaimed, 'because I never saw anything like that in the outside world.'

For a while nobody said a thing. They watched the sky. Thousands of stars lit the night with silver trails, caught in a journey of their own. It looked to the group as if the stars raced each other in a riot of joy, through the heavens.

In a dreamy voice, Will interrupted the silence.

'When I was a shrub for all that time, everything was very different.' He paused. The others still looked up in awe. 'I know that sounds obvious, but it isn't in the way you think.'

Will searched for words, and finding them, he went on.

'A tree is fully awake, you know,' he murmured, 'but in a different way to us. They don't know time like we think of time. Each moment is its own special truth and each special truth has its own reward. It could be a new leaf, a gentle breeze, the sun to make your branches soar.' Will sighed.

Rielle looked away from the stars and glanced at Will. What did he mean, she wondered? What did he mean *he had been a shrub?* It was the first time she had heard Will sound content.

'You were a tree? A shrub?' she finally asked, realising that because of the star trails, they had enough light to see each other.

'Yes, I was a kind of shrub,' Will replied wistfully.

Rielle wondered why, or how.

'A tree thinks; it really does.' Will said the last bit as if explaining something that was important for them to understand. 'It just doesn't think like us. It has friends and it feels pain, and each creature that visits stops by for a reason.' He sighed. 'I was never more carefree or more at peace.' He stopped speaking. The silence held them like a warm, welcome hand.

'Anyway,' Will continued in a gruffer tone, clearing his throat as if there was something caught there, 'when I was a shrub, I thought I could see the star trails because that's something that trees can do. Standing here now, I see it must be something to do with Wish.'

Will paused and then went on. 'I used to watch star trails stream through the sky, and although my feet were buried in the ground, it would make me feel as if I could fly.'

'Oh,' Rielle breathed, 'how beautiful.' Without thinking, she placed a hand on Will's arm but he quickly brushed her off. Rielle ignored Will's snub. Her curiosity was ignited. *He was now a person just like her, but he had been a small tree? Strange things happened in Wish!*

Pud did a funny thing then. He sneezed happily, then bumped into Will and placed his nose on Will's hand. Will was surprised. Before he knew what he was doing, he patted Pud on the face, but he did it as if it was something new and as if patting a dog was a strange thing to do. Pud thumped his tail hard on the ground and gently licked Will's hand, before going back to stand with Rielle.

'What... what's his name?' Will asked.

'It's Pud,' Rielle replied with a smile. 'It rhymes with spud.'

Once again the group reflected on the lights in the sky. Rielle broke the silence. 'I've never seen anything like it. I didn't realise that stars left such bright, beautiful trails. It must mean something, but maybe we'll never know.'

Will turned and looked at her then, pausing in such a way that made Rielle smile curiously at him.

'Stars are in our blood,' he boldly stated.

'What do you mean, in our blood?' Rielle whispered. Shivers shot across her brow.

Will hooded his eyes. 'We are star-stuff,' he mumbled, then shrugged irritably, and turned away.

'Yes, well,' Bibs interrupted, 'I must say it is very good luck to have them, because they've given us some light to see each other by.'

'Then let's go,' complained little Bobs as he peered around at the dark shadows, 'please, let's go!'

Reluctantly Will tore his eyes from the mesmerising sky.

'He's right. By the stars I can find the way. Let's go.'

'Do you think the tower's far now?' asked Rielle, as she and Pud began to follow.

'No,' Will replied cautiously, 'no, not far, but this part may be tricky. We mustn't take anything for granted.'

Rielle.... Rielle... Rielle...

'What was that?' Will gasped.

'I don't know,' Rielle rejoined, 'I would love to know, but I have no idea who it is!'

Rielle... Rielle... Rielle...

Will stopped and turned to stare at Rielle. 'Do voices call you in the night all the time?' His tone was urgent, afraid.

'No, not just the night,' Rielle replied. 'That voice has been calling me, whispering to me for days.'

Will gripped her arm. 'Does it call you only in Wish?'

'No,' Rielle wondered at his panic-stricken voice. 'No, it was calling me in the outside world, and then I also heard it when we were in the forest, and now it's followed me here.'

'You have no idea who it is?' Will grilled her.

'No, I don't, but it does seem to whisper to me when, well…. '

'What? When does it whisper to you, Rielle? Think!' Will still held her arm and his voice grew stranger.

'Well, actually, I have been thinking about it,' Rielle replied cautiously, 'and, well, it seems to say my name when something is… is,' she hesitated to say the words out loud, *'going to happen,'* she finished. She looked at Will and by the light of the stars she watched his face become tight with fear.

Will shuddered. His voice became steely. He looked around.

'Something?' he asked. 'What kind of something?'

Pud whined. Leaves rustled overhead. A chill gust of air seeped through the almond trees. Pud sniffed. There was something in the air but it wasn't too close. He whined, then growled.

'I want to go home,' sniffled little Bobs.

'There, there, hush now,' Bibs tried to comfort him, 'soon we'll be safe inside that tower.'

'What kind of something?' Will confronted Rielle.

Rielle! Rielle! Rielle!

A roar of wind shook the trees around them.

'We have to get out of this orchard and into the tower,' Rielle cried urgently. 'The wind is rising and it's coming to get *us*.'

'I see,' Will snapped. 'You mean to tell me that someone calls your name just before something *bad* happens?'

He had barely finished speaking when the wind roared toward them like a catastrophe: blacker, darker, denser than the night, swooping, driven, maddened, toward them!

'This way,' bellowed Bibs, 'this way! I can find the tower, I know I can!'

Wailing like a tortured soul, the wind tyrannised the trees.

Will grabbed Rielle's hand just as the entire orchard erupted, and hauled her after Bibs and little Bobs. Pud took her other hand gently in his mouth, and like hell-bound toys they did their best to outrun the coming outrage in the dark.

CHAPTER 18

The Gathering

Cradling the Wand of Time, Old strode calmly into the warmth and light of the Tower of Dreams. As he approached the gathering, nothing in his manner revealed that he had just fought for his life.

Old grasped Oobaat's hand, recognising him despite his human shape. Then, turning to Hope, he smiled joyfully up at him. It wasn't until he was by their sides that the others saw the tears of elation in his eyes. For breathless moments, no one spoke.

'Number One,' Old finally breathed, 'Eno On.' He paused as if the emotion were greater than his body could contain. 'Number Nine, Enin On. I dreamed often that this moment might come.'

Joyously, without reserve, Hope and Oobaat hugged their small brother.

The unicorns stood by and silently rejoiced.

Hope stepped back and looked quizzically at Old. His voice was agitated.

'You have been in battle with *him*, am I right?'

'Yes, we battled,' Old replied. 'I escaped.' He glanced

at the gathering with an easy grin. 'I could not die before I was led to the others, my own kind, at last!'

'Led?' Coraggio interrupted. 'Led?'

Old bowed his head in reverence to the unicorn. 'Yes,' he replied, 'a girl and her dog. From her I learned that both Oobaat and Hope lived. I also learned where they might be.'

Benny stepped from the herd. 'Rielle! You do speak of Rielle, am I right?'

Old beamed. 'Yes, Rielle,' he replied quickly.

'Where is she? Is she here with you?' Benny trotted to the doorway and looked outside. He turned back to Old. 'Where is she? Please tell us. We need to know if she's alright.'

'Ah,' Old shook his head slowly, looking sadly at Benny. 'I lost them. I told them run. Neves On brought the wind and the fury. I left them and went to do battle.'

'The wind? So it's true!' Oobaat paced the hall. 'Neves On rules the wind and it does evil for him. We suspected that. But now we have further proof.' He sighed, gazing steely-eyed at the gathering.

Old held up a hand. 'I have much bad news still to tell.'

All eyes watched him. The unicorns leaned forward with grim foreknowledge. Oobaat and Hope stood tall as if suspecting to receive a blow, and Far huddled breathlessly under Hope's collar.

Old looked around. He faced Candela and Coraggio as if the news was expressly for them. Taking a deep breath he placed the Wand of Time in both hands like an offering before he spoke.

'Neves On, Number Seven of the First Ones,' he began

hesitantly, 'holds and wields, against her will, the unicorn wand, the Staff of the Unimaginable.'

The herd trilled loudly. Their greatest fear was confirmed!

'We suspected this was so,' Oobaat whispered to Old, 'but now we have proof.' A weighty silence passed through the gathering as the hall filled with sorrow.

Unexpectedly, the three wands held by First Ones began to hum as if they, alone, knew what to say. Their voices rose, in a harmony of three, softly, so softly, in searching for their sister wand.

Destiny we are seeking
The Truth of Time
We are now meeting

With power earned
All tasks are not done
The day has come

Together, forward
A battle to be had
A battle to be won

With the Staff of Life
With the Wand of Faith
With the Wand of Time

Moon, Stars, Sun and Sky
Beyond, beneath
Below, above

Unicorn
First Ones
Unite as one!

After the last whisper from the wands had settled throughout the hall, Coraggio faced Old.

'We thank you, and cordially greet you, Number Twenty Three, Eerht Ytnewt On. Although it brings us great concern, we are extremely grateful for your news.'

The herd nodded and bowed their heads to Old.

'We must find Rielle,' Benny urged again, breaking the mood, 'now that we know for sure she's out there somewhere in Wish.'

Old turned to Benny. 'The girl travels with her dog and also two *Imperial Guard* Snails,' he announced. 'All is not lost. They are with Bibs and little Bobs.'

Coraggio and Oobaat glanced at each other.

'Bibs and little Bobs?' Oobaat quizzed. 'But we told the snails not to come to Wish. I told them we didn't need their help. What the blazes is going on? Why on earth would they disobey? Bibs understands the danger!'

Old shrugged. 'Snails met us on the shores of this place.'

'It doesn't matter how or why,' Candela trilled, 'if Bibs is with Rielle, then, between him and the dog, she should still be alright.'

'Yes, it's true,' Oobaat pondered, 'Bibs may act silly at times, but he's proven to be a clever chap and worthy of the title *Imperial Guard*. Nevertheless, we must find her! Otherwise she is at the sorcerer's mercy.' Oobaat's eyes pierced the gathering. 'But we must be careful. Neves On must not discover that the entire Lilifel is in Wish.'

Benny tossed his mane and struck a hoof to the ground.

'I must go. I must start looking for Rielle,' he urged. 'It's *me* he's trying to bring to Wish, after all. I have to find her.' He ignored a look from Candela. 'In his wildest dreams, the sorcerer would never believe the *entire* herd would come to Wish!'

'Yes,' Hope agreed, 'it's true. There's no reason Neves On would suspect such a thing.'

'Do not underestimate!' Old boomed. 'He is cunning and crazed.' Old paused and sighed. 'He has broken the Bridge of the Long Forgotten - the bridge I made with these own hands.' Old stared with anguish at the others. 'He broke the *Truth of Time!*'

'Ah, I see.' Hope spoke quietly, yet his manner didn't hide his rage. 'I see. Not only did he dare to steal the Staff of the Unimaginable, but he uses her to unravel our power and to break the promises and the gifts we have made.'

'Then he is more dangerous yet,' Coraggio growled, shaking his mane. 'He dares to break all the laws, even as he dares to defile the unicorn wand. He may well know that he has drawn the whole herd here.'

'No,' Old interrupted, pondering, 'no, I have thought again. I have just fought with him. He does not know this thing.' He paused and heaved a sigh. 'But, he said a human might help him to kill a unicorn.' Old grimaced and glared. 'Then he threatened to find my cave and steal the *Gold of Time.*'

'Not gold,' Hope barked. 'If he finds your gold then we may be done for! We might fight and fight and never win. What's worse, with gold and the wand he wields, he could become so powerful as to overcome us all. It may take aeons before we recover, to the harm of the forest and the outside world.' He turned to Old. 'Does he know where your caves are? Where the gold is?'

Old thought hard. 'I think not. I think protection is still at work. I think if he knew he would have stolen it already.'

'And yet he knows you *have* gold in your caves,' Hope mused. 'If he hasn't found the gold, then how does he know it exists?'

The hall became quiet.

Far crawled out from under Hope's collar and flapped her wings.

'The wind,' she whispered, 'the wind broke the Bridge of the Long Forgotten. I think the bridge was close to Old's caves. Maybe the wind saw the gold.'

'Maybe,' Coraggio agreed, 'but if that is the case, why hasn't the wind told him exactly where the gold is?'

Small rifts of warm air shifted about the gathering as they stopped speaking.

'Perhaps,' Benny broke the silence, 'perhaps the wind is not a *willing* slave.'

Oobaat nodded. 'I was thinking as much, Benny. Indeed, and if that is true, then the wind understands that it is being wickedly used. There may be some promise after all.'

'The Staff of the Unimaginable - she, too, may have hope,' Old murmured thoughtfully.

Eagerly, all eyes turned to him.

'I asked the Wand of Time to sing,' Old explained,

'during battle, and the unicorn wand flung herself away from Number Seven's hands.'

For the first time, Coraggio stopped looking grim. 'Ah,' he cried, 'she remembered! Despite *his* evil ways, she remembered something of how she was made!'

The herd trilled loudly. The three wands, held by First Ones, hummed.

Oobaat faced the gathering. 'We must assume,' he began, drawing himself to his full height, 'that Number Seven does not know we are all here. He must not learn that we have come to put an end to his evil. Surprise is our best plan.' He paused. 'When Coraggio called upon the Oath of Spirit, Fire, Air, Earth and Water, forcing me to relinquish my role as gatekeeper to the wishing pond, the mighty unicorns were calling on me to wield two wands.'

Oobaat locked eyes with each and every one there. 'Not only was I to wield my own wand, the Staff of Life, but also the Staff of the Unimaginable, on their behalf. But the unicorn wand is not with us now.' He paused. The gathering waited. Decisions were thick in the air.

'As Number One of the First Ones,' Oobaat went on, 'it is my duty to fight. I must fight on behalf of unicorns who will not change their shape, as was pledged at the beginning of time. I must lead as chosen. Battle is how this must be done.'

Hope stood beside Oobaat. Old stepped up to his brothers and stood to Oobaat's other side. The three First Ones turned and faced the herd. They bowed. The herd bowed back.

'We will stand behind you at every turn,' Coraggio

whispered. 'We too, will be fighting, but we will fight with the power from the Ritual of Return.'

First Ones and Unicorns nodded their agreement.

'It is battle, then,' Candela sighed.

'Yes, battle,' Coraggio breathed.

'Then let us find Rielle first,' Benny insisted boldly. All eyes turned to him. 'I know,' he breathed, returning their gaze, 'I know. I must go out there and look for her, since that is exactly what the sorcerer is hoping I will do!'

CHAPTER 19

Friendship true

Rielle ran with burning lungs and aching muscles. Will tugged her along, not letting go of her hand. Pud galloped beside them, as Bibs and little Bobs slid faster than they ever thought they could.

For monstrous reasons of its own, the tempest breathed ice and steel, stretching long, grasping fingers towards them. Then, with jaws that dripped fear, the wind screeched in premature victory, and struck. For terrifying moments it clutched Rielle. Helplessly, Rielle began to fall.

Will rallied. Stopping, he looked the black shadow of the tempest in the eye, then grabbed Rielle's arm with all his strength, and with a mighty shout, he wrenched her free.

Enraged, the wind shrieked at its lost triumph.

Terrified by its fury, impossibly, Bibs picked up speed. Following as fast as they could, the others knew they could not keep the pace up for long. The tempest had boundless energy, and they did not.

'This way!' screeched Bibs, as he swerved out of sight.

Rielle felt herself tugged around by Will as Pud pushed her legs to turn.

Tucked beneath a ledge made by a gigantic fallen tree, there was a hollow that formed a small cave. Silent and hidden, they all crouched there, hoping against hope that the wind would go away.

Sniffing for them like a stray beast, the wind wailed in aggravation. Then, finding their small cave, it buffeted against them for what seemed an endless time. Unable to reach them, the wind turned, maddened, to vent its fury at the almond orchard. Relentlessly it struck with wild revenge and destruction. Finally, its temper spent, like a miracle of quiet, it went away.

The aftermath of silence rang in the group's ears. Uncertainly, they breathed again, shifting nervously by degrees. The hollow in which they hid was dark and freezing.

'Are we all here?' Bibs asked, uneasily.

'I am,' little Bobs whispered. Pud whined.

'Yes,' Will muttered, 'and the girl is too. I dragged her with me.'

Bibs breathed a sigh of relief. 'Good,' he murmured, 'it wouldn't do to have lost anyone.'

'What do we do now?' little Bobs muttered.

'We wait until morning, I think,' Bibs replied quietly, 'in case the wind is waiting to trap us.'

'Until morning?' Rielle gasped.

'That sounds like a good plan,' Will reluctantly agreed. 'We seem to be safe enough here and we have no idea where to go in the dark.'

Rielle's heart still pounded and her throat was tight. *She had been clutched in the grip of the wind. She had felt it breathe ice and evil down her back.* Quaking, Rielle shivered at the memory.

'It's very cold in here,' is all she said.

'Let's just try to get some sleep,' Will suggested. 'Hopefully, in the morning, it won't be far to the tower.'

Little Bobs was already curled inside his shell. By the sound of his breathing he was sound asleep.

'Goodnight, then,' Bibs murmured, 'I'm beat.' In just moments, he, too, began to snore.

Pud curled up by his mistress. It wasn't the first time they had slept in a strange, unknown place that was forced upon them. He nudged Rielle to let her know he was there and then placed a paw onto her shoe. Soon he, too, began to breathe in sleep.

Rielle's mind raced. She wanted to sleep but her thoughts churned. Had it been only that morning that she, Pud and Old had run down from the mountain, then hurtled into the forest and come to Wish? So much had happened since! Chills of fear crawled along her spine. She felt as if the wind had left an angry mark on her. For dreadful moments she felt the way she used to, in the days before she had met Benny the unicorn: lost, sad and alone.

Believing that everyone was asleep, Will surprised her when he spoke.

'You're quite brave,' he whispered to Rielle, 'well, you know, for a girl.'

Rielle was too tired to be annoyed.

'My name's Rielle,' she whispered back, 'and you're brave too… well, you know, for a boy.'

Will smiled in the dark. 'Thank you. My name's Will. Funny how we've just learnt each other's names; it feels like we've known each other for ages.' He paused. 'You felt it didn't you?' he breathed. 'You felt the blackness in that wind?'

Rielle shuddered. 'Yes. It had me for a moment. I have you to thank for saving me. It was very brave of you, Will.' She paused then went on.

'I want to apologise for yelling at you when we first met. You frightened me when we collided and then you didn't seem to care. I know you aren't like that now. Not after you kept a hold on me and helped me escape from whatever that was out there.'

'Nonsense,' Will replied gruffly, 'you run like a champ! Well, for a girl, that is.'

They giggled softly for a shared moment, despite the trouble they found themselves in.

'I must apologise too,' Will confided. 'I was horrible to you. It's just that I've had some strange things happen to me lately.' Will grimaced in the dark.

He sighed and went on. 'When we ran into each other, it was a complete surprise. I didn't know what to expect. I thought I might have to… to…. '

Rielle waited. 'What?' she asked. 'Have to what?'

'I thought I might have to fight,' Will concluded quietly.

'Oh,' Rielle pondered. 'I think I understand,' she finally said. 'I've led a strange life too.'

Will sniffed. 'I can bet you,' he snorted, 'that it hasn't

been nearly as strange as mine!'

'I don't know about that,' Rielle countered. 'I've wandered all over the outside world on my own with just my dog. I've met a snake that changed into a tortoise. I've been to the Tower of Dreams and back. I've been held hostage by a horrible old sorcerer and I've met an entire unicorn herd!' She waited for Will to comment, but he said nothing.

For a long time the only sounds were the snores from Bibs, little Bobs and Pud.

Rielle finally decided that Will, too, had gone to sleep. She couldn't blame him for being tired; they had been through a lot since they'd first met. As the dark settled around her, she began to think of Old. Was he alright? Would she ever see her friend again? Her heart sank. She decided that she had better try to sleep.

'So,' Will suddenly muttered, 'so, you say you've met the unicorn herd?'

'Yes,' Rielle was surprised by the sad tone of his voice. 'Do you know them?' she asked eagerly.

Will sighed. 'In a way,' he mumbled.

'They're wonderful, aren't they?' Rielle smiled with memories. 'My best friend in the whole world, after Pud that is… is Benny, the little unicorn. Do you know him?'

'No, I don't really know him,' Will replied uncertainly.

'Then you must know Candela and Coraggio at least?' Rielle asked, surprised.

For a long time Will sat in silence. Finally he replied.

'You might as well know the truth, Rielle. About me… and, well, the unicorns.'

Rielle waited. She only had good memories of the unicorn herd. She half expected him to tell a similar story to hers.

Will coughed. Rielle sensed his hesitation.

'You'll hate me after I tell you,' Will began, 'but you just thanked me for saving your life.' He sighed ruefully. 'I think I owe it to you to tell you the truth. That way you can decide for yourself if you still want to be my friend.'

'I won't hate you,' Rielle giggled.

Will stopped her with his sharp tone. 'You might or might not, but I can't change the truth!' He paused. 'You should know the truth, Rielle.'

'Don't tell me then, if you think it's so bad,' Rielle retorted. 'I lost a friend today, and I'm already sad.'

'The friend you need Hope for?' Will asked kindly.

'Yes, he was looking for Hope, so I thought if I found Hope, perhaps Hope could help us get him back.'

'From where?' Will asked.

Rielle shuddered so hard that Will felt it.

'From where?' he asked again, this time with concern.

Pud woke and nudged Rielle so she would feel safe. Settling himself again, Pud pretended to go back to sleep.

Rielle took a deep breath. 'From the horrible sorcerer I met last time I was in Wish,' she replied quietly. 'He chased and challenged us on a hilltop today. I'm sure it was him. He looked different, but it was the exact voice that I remembered from before.'

Gasping at the news, Will gripped Rielle's arm tightly

before quickly letting go. 'You have *met* this sorcerer?' he asked urgently.

'Yes,' Rielle replied cautiously. 'Last time Pud and I came to Wish, the sorcerer tried to take me hostage. It wasn't me he wanted, though.' Her voice became haunted. 'He was trying to lure Benny, my unicorn friend.'

'So,' Will breathed in a pensive tone, 'he still wants to kill a unicorn, after all this time?'

'You know of him?' Rielle gasped, surprised.

'Yes.' Will hesitated. 'Yes, Rielle. Here in Wish, they call him the Sorcerer of Great Contempt.' Will paused with heavy foreboding. Gently, he reached out and took Rielle's hand. 'If you still want to be my friend,' he said, 'there's a lot I need to tell you, Rielle.'

'About how you know the unicorns and how you know of the sorcerer?' Rielle's voice quivered as she asked. Suddenly she knew there was a lot more to Will than met the eye.

'Yes,' Will replied unhappily as he let go of her hand, 'and now is as good a time as any, I suppose, to tell you my story and how it all began. Are you ready to hear it, Rielle?'

Rielle thought of Old and the unicorns, and drew strength from knowing them. She looked squarely at Will in the dim light. Deep down, she knew that Will would need a friend now. Her heart clouded and her throat grew tight, but she was determined to be brave no matter what she heard. After all, Will had saved her life. He couldn't be *all* bad, could he?

'Alright,' she whispered uncertainly, 'alright. I'm not sleepy. I'm listening, Will, but I will be honest with you; I'm a little afraid of what you'll tell me.'

Pud sat up fully awake. Like a statue, he sat by his mistress, whilst Will told them the truth of his story from the very beginning.

CHAPTER 20

Together we stand our little band

In the hall of the Tower of Dreams, Old turned to Benny. 'If you search for Rielle,' he proclaimed, 'I wish to help. It is me who told her run.'

Benny looked gratefully at the First One. 'I would like that, Eerht Ytnewt On,' he replied. 'It would ease the burden if you came along.'

'Call me Old,' Number Twenty Three of the First Ones stated firmly. Seeing the surprised look in Hope and Oobaat's eyes, Old chuckled. 'Rielle named me this, and I am fond of it,' he explained simply.

Hope and Oobaat smiled and nodded. Their brother had always been different.

Coraggio strode to stand by Benny. 'I'm not fully comfortable with this idea. It might be better if I went instead.'

Benny shook his head. 'No! If the sorcerer sees any unicorn other than me, he might become suspicious. It *must* be me, can't you see? He's expecting it to be me. After all, he knows I'm the one who looks out for Rielle.' He noticed the look of warning on the faces of the herd.

'I'll be careful, I promise, but if anything happens to me, you know I'll return eventually somehow.'

Coraggio pondered before nodding. 'Go then, hesitate no longer. Perhaps it's best if you leave in the dark.'

He turned to Old. 'Thank you Number Twenty Three,' he breathed, 'it will be easier knowing that young Benny has a First One and the Wand of Time close by him now. Take care, both of you, take good care. We will see you when you return safely with the girl, her dog and the snails. Remember you are shielded by the *Ritual of Return*.'

Old and Benny bowed to the gathering. Solemnly, they strode to the entrance of the tower. Looking back just once, they stepped outside into the darkness. In their hearts, they searched for Rielle.

The night shifted nervously. Strange flutters of a swift, sudden breeze rustled the leaves of the almond trees as the air gusted with hints of ice. All was not right.

Old wondered about his lost cake tin, made from gold, and also the golden cloth to wrap the wand. He frowned. He tried to remember where he had dropped them and hoped they hadn't fallen into the sorcerer's clutches. Pausing, Old sniffed the air.

He and Benny glanced tellingly at each other under the light of the stars. Wordless, they strode further into the night, listening carefully for unusual sounds. Softening their strides, Old and Benny remained unheard.

Inside the tower, Candela faced Oobaat and Hope.

'Number Twenty Three said the sorcerer would use a human to find us.'

Hope reflected. 'That makes me wonder. I'm thinking it could mean either of two things. He may have meant by trapping Rielle and therefore luring Benny, but there might be something else.' He looked up from under his eyebrows questioningly. Taking a deep breath, as if he almost didn't dare to broach the subject, he peered thoughtfully at Candela.

'What do you remember of that human male... you know the one... the boy who helped the sorcerer try to harm you, long ago? Would he, by some chance, be named Will?'

Coraggio made a shrewd face. 'How could we forget? Yes, indeed,' he replied, 'we know of Will. Will came into our lives a long, long time ago, just as you say. In fact, strangely, we met him again just after we arrived in Wish, this very day.'

'But that's impossible,' Hope declared. 'Will is in my chambers at this moment, recovering from grave illness and lying in bed!'

'It *was* Willful James we met, I assure you,' Candela responded quietly, 'and apart from signs of wear and tear, he looked hale and hearty.'

'Impossible!' Hope repeated. 'Unless....' he frowned.

Popping out from under Hope's collar, Far flew around his head then finished the sentence for him. 'Unless Will found the Sixteenth Door!'

Hope looked intently at the gathering. 'Excuse me just one moment,' he cried. Hitting the floor with the Wand of Faith, he was gone. Moments later Hope returned.

'Far is right,' he proclaimed. 'By some strange luck, or misfortune, Will has found the Sixteenth Door!' He looked aghast. 'Do you know what this means? Not only is Will now at large, but since he has seen you,' he looked pointedly at the herd, 'and *you*, Oobaat, then if Neves On should find and question him, Will may have no control of his answers!'

Oobaat paced; a glowering frown spread over his face.

'Neves On could find out we are here, and quickly deduce what is going on!'

'What is this Sixteenth Door?' Coraggio asked sternly, disturbed by Hope's obvious distress.

Hope nodded. Pensively, he prepared a reply.

'The Tower of Dreams has many secrets.' He paused, as if about to share a precious confidence, difficult to describe. 'It is an exalted place, loved by all who live within its walls.' He made a wry face. 'For many who visit, however, it hides different truths. Some come here and see no one, some see monsters hiding and so they run away, yet others see only mirrors or statues and nothing that lives or breathes. For others it is a tranquil place, filled with friends and joy.' Hope smiled at the herd as they nodded and murmured. 'I see that you understand.'

He went on. 'Long ago, when the Tower of Dreams was created, its maker thought long and hard and built into the framework, hidden doors, veiled tunnels and private passages. Only two of us now living in the tower know of them all, and I am one of those two.'

'And the other who knows them?' Oobaat questioned.

Far flew to sit on Hope's shoulder. 'It's me,' she replied bashfully to the room of expectant faces.

'Ah, Hope's butterfly,' Candela sighed, as if it made great, good sense.

'How did Will find this Sixteenth Door?' Oobaat pressed.

Hope pondered for a moment. 'Perhaps,' he mused, 'perhaps the door found *him*.' He looked up sternly. 'The door has never revealed itself to anyone but me. I concealed my other door today, and locked my windows with pots of boiling moat mud so Will would be safe. I closed the Sixteenth door fast when Far, Flightlord and I came to meet you. I heard the latch shut firmly.'

Thoughtfully, he brushed the Wand of Faith while he considered. The wand hummed for a moment and then became quiet.

'I heard the latch shut too,' Far confirmed.

With a puzzled frown, Hope nodded, speaking slowly. 'The only way that Will could have found the door is if it was open.'

'What are you getting at?' Coraggio asked.

'Well,' Hope muttered, 'when the door is shut, it becomes a part of the wall. It is impossible to see. In fact, in the beginning, I often forgot it was there and now I use it only when I choose to conceal my movements in and out of the tower.'

'So what are you saying?' Candela queried. 'Are you telling us that the door opened *itself*? Are you telling us that this sixteenth door is special in some way?' She squinted at Hope as if a deeper understanding were dawning on her. 'Enin On,' Candela continued, 'are you saying that this door *lured* Will out from the tower for reasons of its own?'

Hope stopped pacing. 'Yes,' he announced, 'that's exactly what I'm saying.'

'So how or why would a door that remains hidden in

your chambers do that?' Oobaat asked with a worried face.

'I'm not sure,' Hope replied.

Candela marched in front of the gathering. 'Is there a remote chance that this is the sorcerer's doing? I understood he could not, on pain of death, enter the tower.' She turned and looked at Coraggio. 'Is it possible for him to enter the tower somehow?'

'No,' Coraggio stated. He continued with a glint in his eye. 'There is no way, even with the Staff of the Unimaginable, that he can break the tower's taboos. The tower has laws much mightier and everlasting than anything, anywhere! No one is that powerful and not one wand, not even the unicorn wand, could break those laws.' He studied the members of the gathering. 'However, I have another idea,' he whispered, in a knowing voice.

The herd shuffled. Far waited, and so did Oobaat and Hope.

...

Benny and Old walked silently through the deep of night, aware of each noise and gust of air.

'There is strangeness in this orchard,' Old breathed, 'a feeling I have felt before, and it is not good.'

'Yes,' Benny whispered, 'I have felt it too.'

They stopped in a wide clearing. Benny and Old both sniffed the air. Old knelt, put his ear to the ground then stood watchfully. Benny sniffed the soil and, in keeping with the silence around them, stood still.

'We are not entirely alone,' Benny whispered as he peered around.

'Trouble stalks,' Old agreed. 'Trouble stalks front and back.'

'I smell a storm,' Benny murmured, 'and my head and horn hurt.'

'Ah, unicorn horns do not lie, so we must go on with care. Tell me when it is more than a twinge,' Old replied.

They walked for a long time without speaking; their eyes, ears and minds were open for the slightest strange thing.

'Look!' Benny tensed. 'Look at that, over there!'

Old gasped and Benny moaned. Sure enough, as remnants of icy wind flitted about them, they could see the orchard by the light of the stars. Countless almond trees lay dying and torn where devastation and madness had ripped them from the ground. Some of them had grown there for thousands of years, but now, discarded leaves rustled underfoot where they were cast aside from tortured, bent limbs.

Benny shook his aching head. 'Do you think *he* is here with us, or am I feeling the evil left behind by this rage?'

'Neves On is close,' Old muttered through gritted teeth, 'as is Rielle. '

'You sense her, then?' Benny breathed. 'I thought so. There's something else, can you tell?'

'I fear we have walked into a trap,' Old whispered, standing tall.

Benny's head began to ache in earnest. 'What do we do now?'

Just then, as if in answer, the sun began to slowly rise with the first pink rush of morning surprise.

CHAPTER 21

Why me?

Inside the log cave, Will leapt up with a start. He sat staring, as if he could see something that wasn't there.

Pud was awake; he'd kept watch through the night. He nudged Rielle insistently, unsure of Will's strange behaviour.

Rielle groaned, grouchy in waking. Grumbling, she reached behind her, pulling Old's cake tin out from under her back. It had dug into her as she slept. Blurry-eyed, the first thing she saw was Will's wide-eyed face.

Puzzled, she sat up. 'Will,' Rielle whispered, 'Will, are you alright?'

What was the matter with Will? What was he watching in that eerie way?

Will continued to stare. Rielle hugged Pud closely. She glanced around the closed, dark den. The snails were gone!

Yawning hugely, Pud tapped her with his cold, wet nose. Rielle patted him as if to reassure them both.

'I wonder where Bibs and little Bobs are?' she whispered. 'If they don't return soon, I'll have to go looking for them.'

Pud whined softly.

'Will?' Rielle asked again, not sure whether she should shake him or leave him alone. 'He's beginning to give me the creeps,' she breathed to Pud. 'Is he awake or asleep?' She waved a hand in front of Will's eyes, but he didn't blink. 'I think he's doing some kind of sleepwalking,' she murmured, 'only sitting.'

She considered what to do next, but in order to leave the tiny, cramped cave she would have to climb over Will, and she didn't fancy that. He was scaring her. Her thoughts turned to Old. With a lump in her throat she thought of Old's cheery smile, his interesting outbursts, and his flashes of wisdom.

Was Old alright? Would he survive a clash with the sorcerer?

Rielle shivered. Memories of the Sorcerer of Great Contempt crossed her mind. She and Pud had encountered him the last time they had been in Wish. At the thought, a shadow filled her heart. The sorcerer was terrifying and evil.

She glanced at Will. It was hard to imagine that she had befriended someone who knew the sorcerer. It was hard to believe that the things Will had told about himself were true.

Will had tried to shoot a unicorn!

Rielle loved the unicorns. They had put the star-scar of protection on her brow and, in so doing, had made her almost one of them. She had a special bond with Benny, the little unicorn. After all, Benny had risked his life to find Hope for her just so he might learn if Rielle still had her dreams.

Then, best of all, Benny had revealed the riddle of unicorns... the words she could say if she felt alone or afraid.

Truth will find me
I have no fear
I have found the unicorn.

Things had changed for her after that. She had never felt completely alone, sad or lost, since. *Believe in yourself,* Benny had told her, *you are precious, and unique, and never alone.*

Unicorns were pure love; Rielle understood that. They were the truest and most powerful creatures ever to be! She sighed. She wasn't sure how to be with Will now, but Will had saved her life. He had pulled her from the jaws of the wind when, driven by evil, it breathed ice down her back. Her neck still felt its touch. She shivered and took a deep breath.

Rielle wanted Will to be a good person; she really did. His ridiculous hat, with the feather sticking out of it, lay on the ground near his feet. Oddly, the hat moved her.

Was Will a bad person who had become good, or a good person who had been led astray? Perhaps... perhaps when you were born to a king, it might make you behave in certain ways, leading you to believe that you could do certain things. Perhaps, if you behaved badly, it might take something drastic to make you realise the kind of things that you did. And perhaps there was no such thing as a person who was all good or all bad, after all. Could it be that there was a big mix of all sorts of things inside everyone, and like a jigsaw puzzle, they had to find a place for the pieces so they all fit?

Hazy light filtered into the hollow.

Will groaned and shut his eyes. 'Go away,' he murmured, 'go away and leave me alone. I don't want to be like you. Do you hear me?' he cried, swishing his hands around his head. 'I don't want to be like you!'

Rielle gasped and held Pud tight. A flash of pain burst through her head. She put her hand up to her star-scar but it was only fleetingly warm to touch. The pain left, but she was afraid in case it returned. If it did, that meant only one thing… evil lurked too closely.

'Should I wake him?' she whispered to Pud. Pud nudged her.

'I'm awake,' Will sighed, 'I'm awake now.' He looked cautiously at Rielle, his blue eyes clouded. *Would she still be his friend? He had told her all his secrets!*

'Oh,' Rielle replied, trying not to let him see her concern, 'I thought you were doing some kind of sleepwalking, except without the walking part. You've, well… been sitting up with your eyes open for quite some time.'

Will passed a hand across his brow. 'Have I?' he asked. He did his best to smile. He looked cautiously at Rielle, as if he wanted to hide. 'I thought I was somewhere else. I thought I was talking with someone else. I must have been in a dream.'

Rielle smiled back. Despite what Will had told her about himself, her heart went out to him. He seemed so unhappy, and she, too, had once been like that.

Will looked intensely at her as if he had to say something or burst.

'There is a voice that talks to me in the dark,' he declared, 'and I'm afraid to give it a name.' He paused. 'That's why, well, that's why I asked about the voice that calls to *you*,' he stammered. 'I wondered if it might be the same voice I hear in my dreams. But I don't believe it is,' he finished, despondently.

At that moment Bibs and little Bobs rolled with a thud and a clump into the cave and cheerfully looked around.

'You should see it out there,' little Bobs yelled, 'it's a mess!'

'A mess?' Rielle frowned. 'What do you mean?'

'Huh!' Bibs shook his head importantly. 'Trees ripped up, branches everywhere, stuff all over the place. It's a mess!'

'We found food, though!' little Bobs cried.

Rielle realised how hungry she was. She and Pud hadn't eaten since they'd shared tea and cake with Old in his den.

'We had breakfast, but we didn't bring any back. We didn't think you'd like the things we eat,' Bibs apologised, 'but at least the wind isn't there anymore, just lots of logs and broken stuff.'

'That's terrible news!' Rielle gasped. 'The orchard in the Valley of Possibility has been there forever. Do you mean to say that it's *all* destroyed?'

'No, not all, just as far as we could see,' little Bobs stated.

Rielle wanted to cry. All those beautiful trees with their pink and white blooms and the delicious smell that the blossoms made - broken, crushed and ruined on the ground. Angry with whatever had driven the wind and caused the waste, Rielle picked up Old's cake tin and cradled it in her arms as if somehow, by doing so, she would be protected.

'What's that?' Will asked. He had become quiet when the snails had returned but now he couldn't take his eyes off the cake tin.

Rielle held the cake tin out from herself. 'It's not mine,' she began. 'It belongs to Old. That's my friend who was left behind.'

Will moved closer to her and held out a hand as if to take it.

'Can I have a look?' he asked, with eyes that suddenly sparkled.

'Well, it isn't really mine,' Rielle frowned. 'You have to give it back.'

'Of course,' Will agreed, but he looked at the cake tin as if he'd never seen anything more beautiful.

Reluctantly, Rielle let him take it.

'Gold,' Will whispered almost to himself, 'it's gold, pure gold.' He laughed briefly then shook it. It rattled. 'There's something inside,' he said.

'Oh,' Rielle remembered, 'that would be tea for sadness.'

'Tea for sadness?' Will looked puzzled, but promptly, he removed the lid. He put his hand in and removed a small package.

'Is this tea for sadness?' he asked, handing it to Rielle. Not waiting for a reply, he peered back into the tin.

Will looked up. 'You know there's something in here!' he exclaimed, and carefully, he drew out a slab of cake.

'But that's impossible,' Rielle gasped, 'there was no cake in there when I looked inside, back in… in Old's den. I mean, we'd eaten it all. There was none left!'

Will took a bite of cake. Then, breaking off a large piece, he handed it to Rielle and gave a small piece to Pud. 'Well there's cake inside now,' he smirked, happily munching, 'and plenty of it!'

Bibs and little Bobs craned their necks, wide-eyed and drooling, as they waited for crumbs to fall to the ground.

'Here,' Will said, feeling sorry for them, 'I bet this is better than whatever it was you found to eat this morning,' and he placed small pieces down for them.

'I wonder how cake got in there,' Rielle queried, after she'd eaten several more slices. 'There was nothing in there except tea for sadness, I'm sure of it.'

She frowned. *What had happened to the golden cloth?* Rielle kept the thought to herself. Just like Old himself, the cake tin was a mystery and a marvel.

'The sun has come up at last,' Bibs interrupted, 'fully up, so we had better go.'

'Yes, we should go.' Will looked thoughtful. 'We need to reach the tower as soon as we can.' He peered at the snails. 'You go first, and we'll follow.'

Bibs and little Bobs made their way easily out from under the log as Will moved over to let Rielle through. She crawled out followed by Pud. Last to leave was Will. Devastation met their eyes.

'Oh,' Rielle gaped in shock, 'this is terrible! I hope it's not the whole orchard!'

'It is not,' a voice said softly behind them.

They all turned. Rielle gasped. Running to them, she hugged Benny, then Old, in a fever of relief.

'I'm so glad to see you both!' she cried.

Will stood to one side watching, as if being an outsider was not new to him. He clutched the cake tin under one arm and watched soberly, as Rielle, Old and Benny reunited. After some moments, Old held Rielle at arm's length and looked enquiringly at her.

Softly, so softly that only Rielle and Benny heard, he muttered, 'Trouble stalks front and back. We must escape.'

Immediately Rielle understood. 'Then we'll follow where you lead,' she whispered, 'but let me introduce you quickly to my new friend.' She turned and gestured to Will. 'This is Will.'

Stiffly Will came forward. He faced Benny and Old as if he were ready to flee.

'Ah,' Old grunted, with a smile, 'at last.' Then reaching over, he gently tugged the cake tin out from under Will's arm.

'Eerht Ytnewt On,' he introduced himself, and, pointing to Benny, 'the unicorn, Benny.' Old bowed, but he had a knowing look even as he did so.

Will nodded seriously as if he were facing a lion's den.

'Oh,' Rielle remembered, 'here, Old, I have your tea for sadness.' And opening the lid to the cake tin, which was empty of cake again, she dropped the small package inside, where it landed with a bump and a thud and settled against the cloth of gold which, somehow, had returned.

Either rhyme or reason

To the expectant faces in the hall, Coraggio recited:

For he who falls and also fails
Yet rises despite hardship and travail
Does hail from Kings and kingdoms far away
Let no hindrance stop his passage
Nor lay him low to halt his steps
Or his destiny in time
Either night or day

'Ah,' Hope nodded sagely, 'of course! That's from the Book of Divination. Well done, Coraggio, Lilifel friend.'

'Yes, well done, indeed!' Oobaat cried.

Candela shook her mane and stood tall. 'Husband, do you believe this is the answer to the mystery of Willful James?'

Coraggio nodded. 'Yes,' he replied, 'but most importantly, I believe it is the answer to Willful James *and* the Sixteenth Door!'

Coraggio peered at the gathering. '*Let no hindrance stop his passage*…. That could answer our questions about the

Sixteenth Door: about why it was possible for Will to see it, and also to find his way through it. *Does hail from Kings and kingdoms far away....* Will has told us he is the son of a king. If that is true, then the rhyme fits.'

The herd nodded, as did the First Ones.

Coraggio continued. 'He came from *far away* to visit Wish all those long years ago, and he *fell and also failed* - shooting at Candela, before wishing to heal her wound and then turning himself into a shrub. Perhaps he will fail again. Who knows? But if he is the one spoken of in the Book of Divination, then there must be *no* hindrance to his passage, so that his *destiny,* and no doubt ours, will be met.' He looked up at the walls and ceiling. 'My heart tells me that this rhyme is Will's, and if destiny is taking place, then the Tower of Dreams will do everything in its power to help it.'

The gathering looked around, as if they knew that the walls and ceilings surrounding them were much more than just a building - more a place that breathed and thought with its own authority.

Into the silence Candela spoke. 'There is another part to this rhyme.'

'Yes,' Coraggio replied, 'indeed there is, and I know it well.'

He recited the first part of the verse again:

For he who falls and also fails
Yet rises despite hardship and travail
Does hail from Kings and kingdoms far away
Let no hindrance stop his passage

Nor lay him low to halt his steps
Or his destiny in time
Either night or day

Coraggio paused before going on.

He addressed Candela. 'This is the next bit that I think you have in mind.'

Lest destiny will not be met
Lest the Truth of Time will not be kept
Where laws and rules must be upheld
For he who fell will fall again
Yet find his place and be set free
By that which flies and friendship true
By humble wand and gentle death too

Beneath, below and above
The rhyme you read must be told
In many score it will unfold
So let no hindrance stop his steps
Or block the path of his tread
For only through the pain of dread
Will justice, honour, and truth, win

'That is the full rhyme as I know it,' Coraggio stated, 'written many thousands of years ago.'

'There is yet one other part to this rhyme,' Candela breathed into the thick silence that followed.

All eyes turned to her.

'Yes,' she explained, 'I was there when it was written,

but the Book of Divination lost four of its pages in the Battle of the First Ones ten thousand years ago, so it is not well known.'

Coraggio stepped forward eagerly. 'Do you remember the missing part?'

The unicorn herd craned their necks, their eyes expectant.

'Yes,' Candela breathed, 'yes, I do.'

She faced the gathering and finished the verse.

Although we as men
Draw breath
And build castles in the air
And spend our time
Fleeing death
Life awaits us
In the wings

Although we as unicorns
Do vow and honour
To protect
And spend our time
Sowing deeds
Life belongs to those we help
And to those in need

Although we as First Ones
Watch the gates of being
And spend our time
In the art of weaving
Life begins in our timely actions

And in our knowledge
From the beginning

And so
Having said
In the end
The challenge lies
For all of us
Not in big
But in little things.

'Ah,' Hope murmured, 'so it is written that men and unicorns and First Ones will come together, in the end, no matter what.'

'Yes,' Oobaat agreed, 'and in the end the challenge will be ... not in big, but little things.'

For a long time, the hall was silent.

'We are all being tested then,' Oobaat finally stated. 'Each and every one of us can take no one thing in life for granted.'

'History shows this to be true,' Hope agreed. 'Perhaps not for unicorns, but men and even First Ones have fallen, like... well, like our brother, the Sorcerer of Great Contempt... and Willful James.'

With shadowed velvet eyes, Candela addressed the gathering.

'Unicorns have never fallen, because we protect ourselves with the Ritual of Return. We *chose* not to have hands and feet so that temptation could not be ours. The Ritual of Return keeps us pure and allows us to serve with truth.'

'Indeed,' Oobaat agreed. He grinned awkwardly before going on. 'Why, as Number One of the First Ones, I prefer to spend my time as a tortoise; it is a much simpler way to be. That way, I am never tempted by my power.'

Hope intervened. 'So, it seems that the tower already knows of Will, and because of that, the Sixteenth Door revealed itself to him. Would you all agree?' Everyone nodded. 'So, we must presume there was a very good reason for him to be lured from my chamber... but I wonder what?'

'We met him in the orchard,' Candela interrupted. 'We could have avoided him, but I felt that destiny had taken a hand and had sent him to us.'

'Of course,' Coraggio cried, 'I believe I have it! Will begged Candela for mercy and forgiveness... after all this time! He made a promise to us, and now it is on his conscience to do the right thing. Don't you see? If the sorcerer should get his clutches onto Will, then because Will met us *when he did*, he promised to walk the path of truth.'

Coraggio beamed. 'If Will had remained in Hope's chambers and then learned that we unicorns were here in Wish, would he have *chosen* to confront us? Would he have *chosen* to beg forgiveness? I think not! Rather, he may have chosen to run away. This way, what looked like an accident may have been the master hand of fate. Will must choose to do the right thing now!'

Hope chuckled. 'And so the Sixteenth Door lured him out of my room and into the almond orchard.' He frowned. 'Why though, has Will not returned to the tower?'

'Perhaps he got lost?' Candela offered.

'Or perhaps he chose to run away because we are here?' Coraggio returned.

'Or,' Hope looked tired suddenly, 'or perhaps he ran into the sorcerer? Perhaps the story in the rhyme continues? To fall again? Can Will find his place and be set free?'

'Time will unfold this part of the divination for us,' Oobaat sighed, 'but for now we must consider how Benny and Number Twenty Three are getting on in their search for Rielle, the dog, and the Imperial Guard.'

'Yes, you're right.' Coraggio nodded. 'Gather around, we must focus on Rielle and Benny and Eerht Ytnewt On, and send our light to bring them home.'

CHAPTER 23

Separation

'We must hurry, but stay calm,' Old whispered furtively to Rielle, Will, Pud and the snails.

Benny nodded. 'My head is aching badly now. Evil is lurking near.'

Even as he said it, Rielle felt the star-scar grow hot on her brow.

'I see that you feel it,' Benny noticed. 'We have no time to lose, so follow me.' He led the way. They trekked as quietly as they could before Benny finally turned to Rielle. 'I must tell you,' he smiled, 'that Far is safe and back at home.'

Seeing Rielle's face light up with joy, Old held a finger to his mouth to bid her hush. 'Rejoice quietly,' he whispered. 'You should know there is a plot to trap us.' He paused and eyed a massive fallen tree as something rustled its broken branches. But it was just a bird.

Old looked thoughtfully at Rielle. 'The butterfly was seized by the wind, but only to lure you back into Wish.'

Rielle's eyes opened wide.

'Do not fear,' Old went on, 'the sorcerer wanted this.

He does not want *you*, Rielle; he wants the little unicorn. That was his plan all along.'

'So,' Will interrupted, as he listened in, 'so he still wants to catch a unicorn?' He turned to Benny. 'He planned to capture Rielle and lure you out from hiding? Why would the herd send you out here alone, when … '

'Hush,' Old growled, 'hush! Be quiet and say no more!'

Old and Benny peered around at the very shadows on the ground. Strewn broken and bent branches gave the ruined orchard a sinister air.

Will frowned. 'What did I say wrong?' he asked. 'I was only … '

Old turned on him, and this time he hit the ground with the Wand of Time to make his point.

'Enough! You have spoken too much. Hold your tongue!'

Will gaped. 'Alright,' he complained, 'I see I'm not welcome here.' Without another word, he stormed away from the group.

'Will,' Rielle urged, 'come back, don't go. It isn't safe to be on your own.'

'Shh,' Benny cautioned, 'shh.'

'What's that noise?' little Bobs' voice quivered.

The group listened, but Rielle continued to watch Will as he walked away. Suddenly both she and Benny let out a cry. Rielle put her hand to her brow and Benny winced, his eyes clouded with pain.

'What noise?' Bibs asked.

'*That* noise,' little Bobs replied.

And then they could all hear it. Chilling laughter sailed toward them.

Pud pushed himself close to Rielle, protecting her. The group drew their breaths.

'Prepare to fight or run,' Old growled.

Will, too, heard the laughter as he sauntered away from the others. His blood ran cold. Promptly, forgetting his sulks, he turned tail and began bolting back to the group.

'*Where are you going, Willful James?*' Number Seven of the First Ones, Neves On, the Sorcerer of Great Contempt, blocked Will's path like dark, ravenous terror.

Old turned to Benny. 'Run,' he urged under his breath, 'run, with the girl, the dog and the snails. Get them back to the tower. Quickly! I have the Wand of Time to help me, now get out of here!'

Benny didn't hesitate. Rielle, Pud and the snails were innocents. He must lead them to safety.

'Rielle,' Old quietly barked as he turned away, 'catch!' He threw the golden cake tin at her. Rielle caught it. Before she could say a word, Old was gone.

'Down here!' Benny breathed as he led them down a steep embankment. At the bottom he urged, 'Run! Run now, like you've never run before!'

The tower wasn't far away. Rielle could see it as she followed Benny. Soon they'd be safe inside its walls! Despite the pain in her head she followed blindly, running as fast as she could. In her mind she kept thinking one thing. *What was going to happen, this time, to Old and to Will?* She clutched the golden cake tin like the treasure that it was.

Scorning hideously, the Sorcerer of Great Contempt loomed largely over Will as Will's mind raced to find ways of escape.

'My friend, Willful James.' Neves On chuckled disturbingly. 'We meet again, face to face. Not when you are sleeping, but while you are wide awake.'

Will gathered his thoughts as he tried to stay calm.

'So,' Will faltered, 'those weren't just dreams, after all?'

'Just dreams?' The sorcerer arched his eyebrows. 'Of course they were not just dreams! Do you think my visits are any less real because you are asleep? You underestimate my abilities, *friend!*'

'What do you want?' Will asked, trying to mask his dread. 'You were never my friend. I don't want anything to do with you!'

The sorcerer paced before Will like a huge agile predator.

Trapped, Will thought he caught a glimpse of Old, but he wasn't sure. It looked like the others had run away. Will hoped they had, even as loneliness welled grimly within him.

The sorcerer stopped pacing. He fixed Will with livid eyes.

'You betrayed me, Willful James,' he hissed. 'You know, don't you, that there is a price to pay?'

A hand of fear grasped Will's heart to squeeze the light from him.

Surely, after all this time, there would be no grudge or debt of any kind.

Will dared to look the sorcerer in the eye, but in doing so, a cloud crossed his mind. Steely panic gripped and tore at his stomach and left him reeling, as if he'd been hit. Terrified, he tore his eyes away, but something evil sat on him and wouldn't go away.

The sorcerer laughed through ugly, grim lips. 'If you

want to leave Wish, Will,' he began in a liquid, enticing voice, 'and go back home again, *I can help you*.'

Quickly Will looked up.

'Ah, I see that's what you'd like,' the sorcerer grinned, 'so the way I see it, if you help *me*, then... well, then I can help *you*.'

Will's mind spun. He wanted to go home, back to where he'd come from, even though he'd been gone for so very long and wasn't sure what he would find.

'Why do I need *you*?' Will retaliated. 'I can find a way home by myself. I don't need you.' He said the words, but doubt gripped and twisted inside him as he spoke.

The sorcerer paced again. 'Let me put it a better way,' he seethed. 'If you don't help me, then I'll make sure you never leave. Is that clear, Willful James?' He stopped pacing and, in the blink of an eye stood directly over Will, daunting him with his darkness and height.

Old could listen to no more. He knew he had to do something before things went too far. 'Enough!' he barked, stepping from the shadows.

The sorcerer turned around. Crooning with grim joy, he leered at Old.

'Ah, it's the little *nothing*, Number Twenty Three, with his trivial wand! Do you expect to save this human?'

Sickened and shaking, Will's head reeled with clinging, bleak thoughts. He wasn't sure what to do. He was helpless against the sorcerer, but he couldn't run and leave Old to fight alone.

Neves On began to snigger. 'I fear that you sent the girl and the unicorn to run away,' he spat, 'but you see,

Eerht Ytnewt On, I don't need them after all, because I have this human to help me with my plans... my old accomplice, Willful James!' He held a hand out toward Old, as if expecting something from him. 'I believe you have something that would be useful to me.'

Old stood his ground. 'I have nothing for you,' he replied calmly, evenly.

'Tut, tut, tell no lies. I know you carry something made from your own precious gold. Am I right?' the sorcerer growled.

'No gold here,' Old answered grimly.

The sorcerer banged the Staff of the Unimaginable into the ground and screamed. 'You have gold, I know you do! I can smell it on you, fool!'

With a swift movement of the white walking wand, he jerked Will cleanly off his feet, flinging him harshly onto the ground in front of Old.

'Bring it to me!' the sorcerer ordered. 'Bring it to me Willful James. Bring me the gold you have both held!'

Gasping in agony, Will looked at Old, his breath rasping in his throat.

'He means the cake tin. Give him the cake tin!'

'It is gone,' Old answered, 'lost.'

'Fool!' the sorcerer shrieked. 'Fool! Now you will learn you have made a mistake. Release the gold,' he bellowed, 'release the gold and make it mine!'

He held out his hands, but the cake tin was long gone. Unwilling though she was, the Staff of the Unimaginable tried to find the cake tin. Sensing no gold, she whimpered miserably.

'I see,' the sorcerer finally breathed in a quiet voice, far more sinister than his screams. 'Clearly, I should have taken the girl and the unicorn, instead of wasting my time here. Well, it's never too late for that plan.' He grinned. 'First let me finish here.'

He raised the white wand, fiendishly grinning at the half-conscious Will.

'Vanquish,' he whispered, with morbid relish.

Old leapt to block the spell, the Wand of Time held high.

'Remember, unicorns made you!' he called to the Staff of the Unimaginable.

For precious seconds, the unicorn wand ignored him. The ground around Will began to burn and sizzle.

Old called again. 'To murder is to kill yourself!'

The Staff of the Unimaginable stopped glowing red.

'Vanquish!' screeched the sorcerer, but the wand he held was fighting a battle of her own, and her indecision made her pause.

'I don't have time for this!' the sorcerer bellowed, and hitting the ground with the white wand, he vanished.

'Stay!' Old bellowed to Will.

Drifting in and out of consciousness, Will barely heard him.

...

The Sorcerer of Great Contempt and Number Twenty Three of the First Ones raced to reach Rielle and Benny - Old to save and warn them - the sorcerer to capture the unicorn and the gold. Seconds flew by in Wish, but the race between the First Ones took place in a land that time forgot, in the mists of their mind's creating. The two First Ones battled, even as each strove to reach the innocent ones first. Grinning devilishly, the sorcerer threw obstacles in Old's way. But Old raced with the Truth of Time, to save the unicorn and the girl.

...

'We're nearly there!' Bibs cried. Soaring above them, the first steeples of the tower reared overhead. It looked as if they could reach up and touch them.

'Don't slow down,' Benny called. 'Whatever you do, don't slow down until we're all inside!'

Almost faltering with exhaustion, and with few reserves left, Rielle ran as she never thought she could. At last, the bridge appeared in front of them.

'Quickly!' Benny hastened, steering Rielle, Pud and the snails before him to reach safety within the tower. The group rushed inside. The Tower of Dreams closed around them.

Protected at last inside the tower, Rielle collapsed against a pillar. Still clutching Old's cake tin, she gasped so hard for breath that she thought her lungs would burst. Bibs and little Bobs limped after her, but once inside, Pud began to howl.

Rielle panicked. 'Where's Benny?' she gasped. Almost crawling, she forced her body to the doorway.

Pud howled again. He and the snails cautiously peeked out.

'Stop there!' a voice called, halting Rielle in her tracks. Old stood outside with a hand held up. 'Stop!' he bellowed.

Rielle realised that he was pointing the Wand of

Time at the golden cake tin. She understood. Turning to place the cake tin safely away from the door, she was met with a wall of white and dozens of velvet eyes. It was the entire unicorn herd! A man stood with them. He stepped forward.

'I'll take that.' He held his hands out to take the cake tin then smiled reassuringly at Rielle's wary look. 'It's alright. We've never met, but you know of me as Hope.'

Relieved, Rielle handed him the cake tin. 'Something's wrong,' she cried. 'Benny didn't come into the tower. Old is out there too!' Without waiting for Hope to answer, Rielle ran back to the doorway. She stifled a cry.

Unbelievably, Benny was being circled by Old and the sorcerer. With wands held high, the First Ones were warding each other off.

'Let him be!' Old growled.

'Ah, now why would I do that?' the sorcerer grinned. 'I am moments away from being free!'

'Not the unicorn,' Old bargained, 'not this little unicorn.' He stood his ground. 'Let the unicorn go... then I will give you gold!'

The sorcerer stopped. With a look of genuine excitement, he paused and let the Staff of the Unimaginable rest by his side.

'You would give me your gold?' he asked warily. 'Is this a trick, Eerht Ytnewt On? Would you dare to trick me?'

Even as the two First Ones locked eyes, Benny slowly - very slowly - began to step backwards toward the tower's doorway.

'A trick?' Old pretended amazement. 'How does one

trick a First One? Especially when he holds the stolen unicorn wand, the white wand, the greatest wand of all time, made from the Tree of Life!'

'Then bring me the gold and do it now!' the sorcerer hissed. He barely concealed the desperation buried in his livid eyes.

'Let the little unicorn go,' Old haggled. 'Let him be free to enter the tower.'

'I don't trust you,' Neves On cried. *'Show me this gold!'*

Rielle turned from the scene outside and looked at Hope standing there with the cake tin. The unicorn herd did not budge, but Rielle saw the looks of concentration and concern in their eyes.

'We must fight him,' Oobaat whispered. 'Number Twenty Three cannot do this alone. Benny's life is at stake and hangs in the balance!'

Oobaat went to take a step, but Hope passed him the cake tin, placing it squarely into his hands.

'No,' Hope replied, 'Neves On must not suspect that either you or the herd are here. Whilst you stand inside this building he will not have a clue. Stick with our plan. We cannot do things half-way. If we want to stop him we must do it well. Stay inside until the best time for battle arrives.'

'This looks like the time,' Oobaat growled. 'Benny is in real trouble. Now is as good a time as any to put an end to this.'

'That would do no good,' Candela intervened, her nostrils flaring. 'If we all show our faces now, he could strike Benny in an instant and for precious moments, until we can revive my son, the Ritual of Return will be broken. Don't you see? We can never attack while he holds a unicorn captive, not in *any* way. While he holds the unicorn wand, he wields the power to destroy the Ritual of Return, but only if he also holds a unicorn hostage. We cannot take that chance.'

Candela did not raise her voice, yet the force of her words lashed the council. 'We *must* wait. The right time will present itself. If Number Seven breaks the ritual, he will have precious moments to escape. That must not happen. Wish is the only place where his evil is contained.'

'Hold the gold,' Hope barked to Oobaat. 'He knows I live here in the tower; he expects me to be here!' Hope turned briefly to the herd. 'I cannot leave Number Twenty Three alone with only the Wand of Time, to fight. Stay here, don't let Neves On see you!' He touched the Wand of Faith to the ground and was gone.

Rielle and Pud held their breaths as they watched the scene outside unfold.

Little Bobs sat round eyed. 'Will he kill us all?' he whispered to Bibs.

Unhappily, remembering his first encounter with the sorcerer, Bibs just shook his head. 'No, little cousin,' he said, 'not while we stay in the tower.'

Little Bobs moaned. 'Does that mean we'll never see the forest again?'

'Of course we'll see the forest again!' Bibs encouraged, and he expected it to be true, but he hid his face from his little cousin as he said it.

Hope appeared in a flash to stand next to Old. The sorcerer turned to confront them both as he grunted a chilling sound.

Slowly, Benny continued to back away.

'So, it seems my brothers are going to betray me once again!' Neves On scorned. 'Don't you see?' he sneered. 'It wouldn't matter if there were more of you, because it is me who holds the greater power!'

Benny was almost inside the tower.

'You hold a stolen wand,' Hope calmly stated, 'and you can never be too sure of something that isn't yours.'

'That's where you're wrong,' the sorcerer seethed. 'I control the unicorn wand now. You know, as well as I do, that the only time she can be reclaimed is if the entire herd were to call her name, on the ninth day of the sixth month, at the moment the Junior Star is formed.'

He laughed shortly. 'That day is not due for another hundred thousand years!' He paused. 'You know, as well as I do, that the unicorns will never, on pain of death, come to Wish together, not even to reclaim their wand! Hah, imagine the destruction I could wreak if they did… they wouldn't dare to take that chance.'

'Do not over-estimate your power,' Old murmured, as he stood ready to fight.

'You bore me!' the sorcerer bellowed, lashing around to check on Benny.

'Are we creeping backwards then?' he breathed quietly. 'Are we sneaking, sneaking, little one?'

Benny stood stock still. The doorway to the tower was just a step away. The power from the herd was so strong that Benny felt the Ritual of Return wrap around him like a glove.

In a movement of lightning daring that made Rielle gasp, Benny flung himself inside the tower's door!

Too late, Neves On raised the Staff of the Unimaginable to smite the little unicorn. Thwarted, he lunged, screeching at Hope and Old.

'*You did this to me, with your idle chat!*' He spewed fire onto the ground and then flung something green and greasy into the air, but Old and Hope hit the ground with their wands and were gone.

Briefly Old appeared inside the tower, and turning to Hope who joined him, he smiled grimly from his half-moon mouth.

'Take care of my gold,' he breathed. 'I must thank you brother, but now I go to salvage Will.'

Rielle wanted to say something, but once again that day, Old was gone.

'Be careful, Old!' she called anyway.

'That was close,' Coraggio breathed, 'too close, Benny.'

Without further ado the unicorns closed their circle. Each and every one came forward to tap Benny with their light-filled horns in reunion and empowerment from the Ritual of Return.

Oobaat gazed, stricken, at Hope. 'What use am I, in human form,' he sighed, 'if I must stay hidden here, and safe?'

Hope turned to Oobaat with a face that mirrored his disillusion and distress. Placing a hand on Oobaat's shoulder, he whispered, 'Remember the verse, brother.'

Although we as First Ones
Watch the gates of being
And spend our time
In the art of weaving
Life begins in our timely actions
And in our knowledge
From the beginning

Hope's voice rumbled over the stone and walls of the Tower of Dreams, as if he were pleading for pity and yet expected none.

CHAPTER 24

Destiny we are meeting

Old raced to reach Will, but it was the sorcerer who arrived first by mere moments. Old did the only thing he could: he hid. Enough near misses had occurred that morning. It would do Will no good if Neves On suspected that Old's purpose was to rescue the young man.

Neves On peered disdainfully down at Will where he lay, half demented with pain and shock.

'Humans!' he scorned. 'Their frailty never ceases to amaze me!' He bent over and taunted Will as if it were a favourite game. 'You are a weak, useless creature, Willful James, but since all else has failed, it is very handy that I didn't kill you, after all.' He prodded Will, who screamed in agony.

'Ah, I see you broke some bones and bits when I threw you? Tut, tut, naughty me. Hmm, I suppose, if I want your help after all, I'd better fix your frail body.' Neves On paused as if wondering whether it was worth his while, but then he pointed the Staff of the Unimaginable at Will and spoke one word, as was his habit when in a hurry.

'Heal!' he spat.

Blue fire leapt from the wand to Will, where it appeared to consume him. The flame withdrew and Will sat up, bewildered, but whole.

It was all that Old could do to contain himself. The young man could not take much more of this!

'Listen to me, Willful James.' The sorcerer grimaced. 'Listen! This is what you are going to do.'

Old watched as Will looked up, confusion mixing with fear in his eyes.

'Willful James,' the sorcerer spoke calmly, 'you are going to remember this later when I need you to.'

Will stood, facing the sorcerer as if he had no choice.

'Good,' Neves On drawled, ponderously tapping the fingers of both hands together, 'good, I see that I have your attention. Now,' he continued, 'Willful James, you are going to make up to me what it is I lost, because of your betrayal all those years ago.' The sorcerer brought his face sickeningly close to Will's as he poked a gnarled, blackened fingernail into Will's chest.

'After you so tiresomely turned into your sympathetic little shrub, the she-unicorn made a wish.' He paused and snarled. 'She wished for all that lovely gold you gave me to simply disappear! Did you know that, Will?'

Number Seven of the First Ones paced up and down.

'Not only did I lose the victory of destroying the Ritual of Return, but I also lost my gold... the gold you gave me, for luring the unicorn to you... to, er, well... kill is such an ugly word.'

He sneered. 'I didn't have the Staff of the Unimaginable then. Silly me... being a First One, and all that, I was still obeying the old laws. We First Ones had made all those ridiculous pacts with unicorns right at the beginning ... the ones in which we swore to protect each other and do goody-goody things.'

The sorcerer pinned Will with molten livid eyes, recollection stirring his anger; his memories bitter, his words unkind.

'I needed someone to do my work for me... so it was wonderful when you charged onto the shores of Wish, with your big sense of self, and your silly jewel-encrusted hat, spouting all that stuff about being a prince, a son of a king, and a warrior to boot!' Neves On laughed shortly and then became grim.

'It was you who decided that you needed a unicorn horn, to make you, well, I'm not sure what you thought it would do, but it was fun letting you believe that you had the slightest hope of controlling unicorn power.' He smirked. 'Ah, you humans play your silly games, and yet you are so frail and childish in so many ways!' His eyes turned into slits as he made a regretful face.

'I have the most powerful of the wands now, and yet, and yet... I have thought about this carefully.' Neves On paused. 'It occurs to me that this unicorn wand may not choose to help me destroy the ones who made it... and I can't take that chance, Willful James. I must be sure when I vanquish a unicorn this time!'

Hidden, Old felt a surge of elation. *There was doubt in Number Seven's mind.* That was good! Although Neves On held the most powerful wand, he was unsure; insecure that the wand was willing to obey him. Old had wondered why the sorcerer had paused on the bridge when Benny was so close and was such an easy target. He grinned. This was a victory of sorts.

'Now, Will,' the Sorcerer of Great Contempt continued, after a lengthy pause, 'let's play a game of make-believe.'

Will frowned. He passed a hand over his forehead, but his eyes were fogged. Will's mind rested in shadows, as if a huge hungry predator owned it.

The sorcerer went on. 'We are going to pretend two things. The first thing we will pretend is that time has not passed us by this thousand years or so.' He cleared his throat, began to speak and then stopped. Squinting, he looked around as if some part of him sensed that they were not alone.

Old shrank back. Quickly, he sent out a thought that cleared the air of his presence.

Shaking his head, the sorcerer continued, but from time to time he peered cautiously about.

'The second thing we are going to pretend is that you still have a desire to possess a unicorn horn.' He stared hard at Will. 'Do you understand what I've said so far?'

Will blinked and furrowed his brow.

Old could not risk Will believing such a thing. In a perilous move that might reveal him, he caught the thought with his own mind, before it could fully sink into Will's brain.

Old dissolved the thought, even as he caught it, but he couldn't be sure how successful he had been. Then Old sent out a thought of his own to Will, asking him to nod.

Will nodded.

'Good,' the sorcerer breathed, 'very good. Now say it! Say the words! It's not enough to nod, my friend. Tell me you understand. I will not risk you letting me down, again!'

Old held his breath. It was risky to continue interfering. This time, the sorcerer might sense his intrusion. He hoped he had done enough. Intervention could hold a hefty price.

Will stared into the sorcerer's eyes. 'Yes,' he agreed, 'yes, I understand. I am going to pretend that I want a unicorn horn.' He stopped and took a deep breath. 'Is that right?' he asked passively.

The sorcerer eyed him carefully. 'Do not mock me, Will,' he whispered. 'This is no game. You are going to *believe* we have gone back in time. You are going to *want* a unicorn horn, for your own, in the here and now!'

Will nodded. 'I understand. I'm not mocking you. Really, I'm not.' He cowered.

Neves On examined him. 'Good,' he hissed, 'now, in order for you to have a unicorn horn, Willful James, what must you do?'

Will's face went blank.

'Think, Will,' the sorcerer urged, 'think!'

Old almost left his place of hiding, but instead, he took another risk. Sending Hope and Oobaat a thought, he implored them for their assistance.

Quickly, Oobaat and Hope responded. Thoughts joined, the three First Ones closed Will's mind and used his mouth to speak. They said the words that the sorcerer wished to hear. Because they were words that came from fabrication, Will remained protected.

'Should I kill a unicorn?' Will asked, his face blank.

'Yes!' the sorcerer cried out. 'Very good, very good, Willful James! Now, be a good boy and pretend we never had this chat. Go on, go away; toddle on back to wherever you want.' He eyed Will coldly. *'When I am ready, I will call on you and you will remember what it is you must do!'*

Promptly, Neves On hit the ground with his stolen walking wand, and was gone.

Will collapsed in a faint and lay, barely breathing, upon the ground.

...

Inside the tower, Hope and Oobaat looked at each other in dismay. They turned to the unicorns.

'These are trying times,' Oobaat sighed, 'when we ourselves must break some rules, and interfere with a human mind, for the greater good.'

Coraggio nodded. He replied, after some thought on the matter.

'It is acceptable this once. Sometimes we, as unicorns, and you as First Ones, must change the course of evil, even though we take the pain and risk upon ourselves.'

'Is Old alright?' Rielle exclaimed unhappily, looking from Hope to Oobaat. 'Is Will alright? Is it very bad for them where they are?'

Benny went to Rielle. She looked helplessly at him.

'Hush, don't fret,' he said, smiling. 'Even though they are your friends, this is not your fight. Remember, Rielle, your job is still to find your dream.'

'My dream?' she asked, shaking her head. 'How can I think about something like that when my friends and the unicorn herd are in trouble?'

'Because,' Benny replied seriously, 'no matter what happens, no matter what, remember what I taught you in the past.'

Rielle looked uncertain. 'You taught me the unicorn prayer and, well, you told me that I wasn't alone and to believe in myself.' She stopped, puzzled. 'How does all that matter now?' she fretted. 'It seems that everything is topsy turvy. Unicorns and First Ones must unite to fight this dread, and my new and old friends might end up... end up... dead!' She finished the sentence in a rush, not willing to burst into frightened tears.

Pud whined and nudged her hard. Old was his friend too, and Will... he also liked Will in a funny kind of way. With wise amber eyes, Pud looked at her as if wishing her confusion would go away.

'Rielle,' Candela strode forward, 'it is more important than ever now, in this dire time, that you, as a human, believe in good and truth and the power of your own heart and mind. That is what Benny is saying, dear.'

'But how can my little thoughts make a difference?' Rielle asked hesitantly. 'It's only me, and I'm no one special. What I mean is... it's not as if I could change the world. You know, like a... a First One or a unicorn.' Rielle blushed, daunted by Candela's beauty and goodness, as usual.

Candela smiled warmly. 'You alone will not change the world,' she replied, 'but you alone can change what's inside you. In that way, my dear, you change the things and the people that you meet.'

Candela nodded, seeing the doubt in Rielle's eyes. 'Yes,' she went on, 'you can. You just have to practise, until what you practise becomes the truth.'

Oobaat knew something of humans from all the wishes he was forced to record when they came to the wishing gate. He felt that he understood how they saw things and also how they felt. He wanted to help Rielle understand.

'If you can,' Oobaat joined in, 'of course you can do more.' He smiled at Rielle, willing her not to be too despondent. He went on.

'If we ask you, then of course you should try to help, but if something is truly out of your hands, Rielle, then that is something you must recognise.'

Rielle nodded gratefully. Her heart lifted a little. She took a deep breath and remembering, she recited:

Truth will find me
I have no fear
I have found the unicorn.

'If I believe in myself, I must follow my heart? If I keep searching for my truth, my dream, then I won't give evil power? Is that what you mean?' Rielle asked.

Hope placed a comforting hand on her shoulder. 'Good girl,' he smiled, 'that's why we created Wish all that time ago. To let humans find their dreams.'

Rielle gaped at him, amazed. 'You *made* Wish?' she gasped.

Hope sighed with the challenge of painful memories clearly written in his eyes. He nodded wistfully.

'It's a long, long story Rielle, but one day perhaps you will learn how unicorns and First Ones came together to make it all possible.'

Rielle shook her head. 'I was told that Wish comes from the minds of humans.'

Hope shrugged grimly. 'It was a *gift*. We gave humans a gift… and then rightly or wrongly, let them make what they would with it.' He paused.

'Except for the wishing ponds and the Tower of Dreams; those are ruled by *other things*.' He smiled warmly at Rielle. 'But it seems that humans are still learning how to use the place. Anyway, as I said, it's a long story for another day.'

Rielle nodded. 'I would like to know, one day.'

Pud placed a paw onto her shoe as little Bobs looked up round-eyed at the human girl he was coming to know.

Bibs sighed and wondered what would happen next. He was still dismayed that Rana had told the truth. Poor little Bobs; he should be safe in the forest. *Where was the tortoise when they had needed him?* Looking up, he noticed Oobaat watching him.

Bibs gasped, as understanding hit him.

'I know who you are,' Bibs spluttered loudly. 'You're Oobaat! You're Oobaat, the gatekeeper!' He paused, frowning. 'Why are you a human man? You're supposed to be a tortoise.'

Rielle gasped as she looked at Oobaat in amazement. *Was this Oobaat the tortoise? Was this the gatekeeper who minded the wishing gate? The last time she had talked with Oobaat, he had been a gigantic snake!*

Everyone stared at Bibs' sudden outburst. Then like a blessed relief, the unicorns, First Ones, Rielle, Pud and little Bobs burst into much-needed peals of laughter at the sincere surprise on Bibs' funny, honest face.

CHAPTER 25

When feathers land

Everything was quiet. There was no pain, no need, and no craving. Will floated contentedly through a pale, stone-washed sky.

A large eagle flew toward him. 'Where are you going?' it cried.

'I'm going home,' Will smiled, 'I'm going home at last!' Will laughed, and the laughter was sweeter than anything he had felt before.

For a while the eagle flew beside him. The sky became a deeper blue. The eagle turned to Will. It looked him kindly in the eye.

'Goodbye Will,' it cried, 'goodbye. I know you'll find your way home one day, but....'

The smile left Will's face. 'But what?' he asked.

The eagle began to turn and fly in another direction. 'I will be seeing you then,' it called, and promptly flew away.

'Don't go,' Will begged, 'please don't go! I need you. I can't find my way alone!'

The sky darkened. Like a spiralling petal, Will began to fall.

Will awoke with a gasp and a stifled scream. He looked around. He lay in a room of gold.

'Where am I?' he croaked. There was no answer.

He sat up. 'Hello,' he whispered. 'Is anyone there?'

Placing his hand down to raise himself, he touched something. It was a feather. The feather was soft. Will picked it up. Its colours of brown and russet glowed and rolled with the changes of the light. Will smiled. Holding the feather carefully, he was surprised when it began to sing.

'Destiny we are keeping,' it trilled.

...

With a jump and a shout, Will awoke from dreaming. Sweat drenched his brow. Inexplicably, the dream within a dream left him shaken. Breathing unevenly, he sat up and looked around. It was the dim of evening.

Old sat several paces away, watching him. He nodded at Will then continued to whittle a small piece of wood.

Will eyed Old warily. He always felt a bit threatened by the First One, although Old showed him nothing but goodness.

In truth, Will wasn't sure what to make of Old's strange black eye-patch, missing ear, short tail, three-toed feet and suction-cupped thumb. Besides, he was still annoyed with the way Old had snatched the golden cake tin back, even though it *was* his.

Will frowned. 'Where am I?' he asked, breaking the silence.

Old said nothing. Will stood up and turned to leave. Old shrugged, put his whittling down, stood, and flicked the Wand of Time at the ground in a casual movement. A small, bright fire began to leap and crackle. Old picked up a battered black pot, threw something dark inside, and placed it on the fire.

'Sit,' he breathed, 'sit and stay, stay and sit.'

Will frowned again, annoyed. 'I have to go,' he murmured, even though he knew it wasn't true.

The last thing that Will remembered was when the Sorcerer of Great Contempt had used the white wand to pick him up and then had thrown him painfully to the ground. Beyond that, Will remembered nothing.

Night was around the corner, but as yet, no stars lit the sky. A chill wind darted around them, but not in a sinister way; it was just a herald of the evening.

Old sniffed the air and then sat. He placed the Wand of Time beside him, balancing her between a rock and the ground. The wand lay, looking like the cane that she was. Despite the darkness, her honey wood glowed golden by the fire. Old ignored Will.

Will wasn't sure what to do.

Slowly, deliberately, Old spoke to his walking wand and then patted her as if she had been good. The kindness of his soft doeskin hands warmed her, and quietly, in a dulcet tone, she began to sing.

Destiny we are seeking
The Truth of Time
We are now meeting

With power earned
All tasks are not done
The day has come

Together
Forward
Moon, Stars, Sun and Sky

Beyond… beyond
Beneath, below
Above

Will whipped around. 'Who's that singing?' he gasped.

Old sighed and looked patiently at him. Casually, he pointed at the Wand of Time as she glowed by the firelight.

Puzzled, Will gaped at Old, then shook his head and began to laugh.

'You don't mean to tell me,' he mocked, 'that you expect me to believe a stick can sing in such a way?'

Old shrugged. Silently, he swiped the wand with one swift movement.

Quickly, as if enjoying the game, she began to sing once more.

Let no darkness
Break the core
Of the boy called up by law

Let no evil win the day
Or steal from Wish and the world
Its frail bits of light and joy

Will gawped, open-mouthed. 'It's a trick,' he stammered. 'You First Ones do all that magic and stuff!'

Old shrugged his shoulders again and this time uttered a single word.

'Truth!' he whispered.

As if she now knew that there were no holds barred, the Wand of Time pealed more loudly and sweetly than ever:

A time must come
For truth to call
A mirror, a lesson, or a fall

Disbelief of the Truth of Time
Brings swift misfortune
And years of pain and contemplation

Believe, Will
Willful James
Believe or reap your sadness and pain

Let the wise ones of the world
Teach you, train you
Heal your wounds

Reject the truth
Then prepare to pay
For the error of your way!

The Wand of Time stopped so suddenly that she left a gap in the night.

Slowly, as Will stood there and Old continued to whittle, small sounds became loud again. A cricket clicking, a branch settling, the knife as it scratched the wood, and Will's own heart in his ears.

For some reason that Will did not understand, the wand's song left him breathless and afraid. It wasn't the type of fear he was accustomed to; it was more a suspicion of the message and its purpose. He peeked over at Old.

The liquid in the black pot boiled. Old calmly lifted the charred old pot from the fire and poured steaming liquid into cups made of plain brown clay.

'What does it mean?' Will whispered, facing the First One.

Not looking up from his pouring, Old pretended ignorance.

'I have made tea for sadness,' he responded coolly. 'Come and sit, sit and stay.'

'No, not that!' Will was impatient now. 'The song, *that* song! What does it mean?'

Old pulled his eye-patch off. He looked Will squarely in the eyes. Brown eyes locked with blue in a moment of truth. The message from the wand struck at Will's very core.

'So, you now believe that she sings alone with no trickery from me?' Old replaced his eye-patch and looked away, much to Will's relief.

Will waited before answering. 'Perhaps,' he finally stuttered. 'I don't know.' He paused and looked sideways at Old. 'After all,' he continued, 'like I said before, it seems that you First Ones do all that magic and stuff.'

Surprising Will, Old laughed cheerily, his free eye lighting up with a look of pure delight.

'What did I say that was so funny?' Will asked, annoyed.

'Not funny; interesting.' Old continued to smile. 'What seems like magic to you is simply common knowledge to me,' he replied.

Will shook his head. 'But,' he stammered, 'you do all that disappearing and stuff and I've seen Hope make things come to him and, well, now you tell me this stick can sing!'

Old sighed and gestured. 'My answer does not change,' he muttered firmly. Then, in a swift movement, Old placed the cups with their steaming liquid down. He leapt to his feet, leaned over and picked up the wand. Holding her in both hands like an offering, and stepping carefully, he went and stood in front of Will.

Will shuffled.

Old looked up at Will, a small smile playing around the edges of his mouth. 'Take this wand,' he whispered commandingly.

Will blinked. Fear flashed through his mind. 'It's just a walking stick,' he stammered.

'Not a stick, Willful James. I wish for you to take the Wand of Time!' Old held the wand out a little closer to where Will stood.

'You all seem to have one of these, um, staffs, or walking wands? You First Ones, I mean.' Will stalled, swallowing a lump in his throat.

Old said nothing.

Will frowned. '*He* also has one, doesn't he? You know who I mean.' He looked around at the dark and the shadows. 'You know, the... that sorcerer.'

'Yes,' Old replied in barely a whisper, 'the Wands from The Circle of Light were made for the First Ones after the beginning of time.'

Will frowned, surprised. 'Surely, surely, the *sorcerer* is not a First One, like... well, like you and Hope?'

Old nodded. 'Yes,' he replied, 'yes, he is indeed a First One.'

'But,' Will fretted, 'he's so different to you and Hope! He's just so different,' he finished lamely.

The Wand of Time was glowing at her centre.

Old nodded. 'Neves On, Number Seven of the First Ones, or the sorcerer, as you call him, has lost his wand,' he replied.

Will was startled. 'But he has a wand like yours and Hope's. I've seen it! Surely you've seen it?'

Old rolled his eyes. 'I will tell you the story after you have shown courage,' he sighed.

'Oh, ha, yes, here goes,' Will stammered. *How difficult can it be*, he wondered, *to hold a magic stick and then give it back?*

Will wiped his sweating palms onto his shirt. Carefully, as if she might be made of glass or break, Will reached out and took the Wand of Time. Copying Old, he also clasped her in his hands like an offering, timidly, and then, enjoying her cool, slender wood, he clamped her in a firmer hold.

At first, nothing happened, but the wand's centre continued to glow. Then, with a tremendous shock of power that almost lifted Will's feet off the ground, the wand began to hum. To Will's amazement, the hum filled not only the forest, but also his mind.

'Good! Enough! Now you are acquainted,' Old

exclaimed abruptly.

Taking the wand out of Will's hands, he quickly went and sat down again, as if he were bored with the whole thing.

Will stood, reeling. He had felt power course through his mind. Power existed that he had only ever imagined.

'What happened?' Will asked eagerly. 'I feel strong!'

'Good,' Old barked, 'now come and sit. I have made tea for sadness, and happy or sad, it is time to sit!'

Jauntily, Will obliged. 'So,' he asked, 'what's this tea for sadness?'

Old grinned. 'Whatever you would like it to be,' he replied as he handed Will a plain clay cup filled to the brim.

Thirsty from his exertion, Will took a sip. 'This is wonderful!' he exclaimed. 'It's just wonderful, this tea for sadness!' He laughed and happily drank it down.

Old looked up with a bemused smile. 'There is some hope for you, Willful James,' he grinned.

Looking at Old as if he wondered why he had ever thought him forbidding, Will asked the question still uppermost in his mind.

'So,' Will pressed, 'what is the story of the sorcerer? And what of the wand you say he lost?'

Will put his cup down and Old refilled it.

Picking up his whittling, and choosing his words with care, Old began to tell the tale.

CHAPTER 26

The White Wand

'Hello Rielle,' Far called. Fluttering from Hope's room, the butterfly joined the goings-on.

'Far!' Rielle burst into happy tears. 'If I could hug you I would,' she gasped.

'Don't cry,' Far begged, landing swiftly on Rielle's shoulder. 'Please don't cry. It wasn't your fault that I went away, but it is my fault that you're here now.'

'It isn't anyone's fault,' Candela protested. 'Far was brought back by evil design and Rielle came to Wish to do the right thing.'

'I was so afraid I'd never see you again.' Rielle sighed, peering at Far on her shoulder. 'I hoped you'd be alright! After all, you are Hope's butterfly.'

'I was born under a lucky star, Rielle. I thought you knew that,' Far giggled.

Rielle sighed again. 'And I was not,' she murmured. 'Seeing you safe and sound is almost too good to be true. It was a terrible whip of wind that took you from that dismal ledge!'

'Yes, yes it was,' Far agreed, 'but we're together again

now and that's all that matters. When all this business is over, I can still help you find your dream.'

Rielle grinned. 'I'd like that! It looks like I'll need all the help I can get to find my dream. It isn't exactly happening quickly, is it?'

Far and Rielle smiled happily at each other. They both looked at Candela. She beamed warmly at them.

'Not all things have *unhappy* endings,' Candela murmured, with a look of knowing in her velvet eye.

Candela walked quietly away then, to gaze outside the doorway of the tower at something it seemed only she could see.

The night rustled in Wish.

'Do you think the trees will grow back?' little Bobs asked Hope.

Hope pondered. 'Do you mean the ones destroyed by the wind? You say it was the wind that tore parts of the almond orchard to shreds.'

'Yes!' Bibs bellowed, listening in. 'It was the blackest, most terrifying thing you've ever seen!'

Little Bobs shuddered. 'It said it was going to eat us.'

Bibs looked at little Bobs. 'No it didn't, it didn't say that.'

'It did!' little Bobs squealed. 'I felt it breathe down my neck and tell me it was going to eat us all!'

'I didn't hear that,' Bibs replied. 'I heard it tell me that it would chase us down and make us run until we turned to dust!'

Bibs and little Bobs stared wide-eyed at each other.

'When it breathed ice down my neck,' Rielle joined in with a shudder, 'it told me that it would capture me and never let me go. It was Will who saved me from its clutches. If he hadn't pulled me free, I dread to think where I'd be now.'

Rielle, Bibs and little Bobs stared at each other with a memory only they shared.

Bibs shuddered. 'I wonder what the wind told Will?'

Silence enveloped the hall.

Suddenly, Candela cried out.

'What is it, my dear?' Coraggio stepped to her side.

'Listen!' she breathed.

Oobaat, Hope and the herd went forward to the doorway of the tower. Looking out, they saw that the dark of night was lit by the gentle caress of star trails. A warm breeze rustled the moat and perfumed almond blossom filled their nostrils.

'I can't hear anything,' Oobaat whispered.

'Listen.' Candela looked at Coraggio. 'Listen. Perhaps only a unicorn can hear this sound.'

So far away it sounded like a whisper, a voice sang:

Alone I lie
Bruised by trouble and pain
With only a memory
Of joy
And my true name
I lie lost
I lie bent
With only a memory
A long gone memory
Of being heaven sent.

The herd and the First Ones stood back sharply and looked at each other as if they had been hit.

'*The Staff of the Unimaginable,*' Candela whispered with a rasp in her throat.

'It's a trap!' Coraggio snapped.

'Perhaps,' Candela answered, 'but she sings somewhere, sad and alone.'

'It's a sure trap,' Oobaat growled. 'The Staff of the Unimaginable is in the clutches of Neves On. There is no way that he would leave her somewhere to sing alone!'

The herd trilled and murmured.

'Unless,' Hope took up the thought, 'unless he wants a unicorn to hear her, and then try to *find* her.'

The herd stomped and rustled as swift thoughts passed from one to another. Benny looked broodingly at Candela as he picked up thoughts from the rest of the herd.

'This can mean either of two things,' he began. 'The Sorcerer of Great Contempt might know we are *all here* in Wish or, if that is still hidden from him, since he knows I am here, he hopes that I will try to rescue her.'

Oobaat paced up and down. 'One thing is for sure,' he growled urgently, 'he is still trying to capture a unicorn!'

'He grows desperate and mad,' Hope rejoined, 'desperate indeed to let the stolen wand sing.'

Pud began to whine restlessly, pacing up and down as if sensing something that the others missed.

'What is it, Pud?' Rielle whispered, afraid. She hunkered down beside him. 'What is it, my faithful friend?'

Pud licked her ear then fretted more. Rielle looked up at the others.

'What is it?' she cried. 'I've never seen him like this before!'

Pud howled lingeringly. His amber eyes stared beyond the doorway of the tower. All eyes followed his.

A shriek filled the night. It froze everyone's blood.

Far dashed headlong and hid in Hope's chamber. Rielle stood, but rested her hand on Pud's head. Pud murmured a deep groan in his throat. Bibs and little Bobs had curled hard into their shells. Rielle looked at the herd. They all shed silent tears. Fearfully, Rielle snapped her head up to look at Hope and Oobaat. Their faces were white and closed.

Grimly, Oobaat broke the silence. 'We must fight now. *Now!*'

Candela stepped away from the doorway of the tower. 'He harms the unicorn wand for daring to sing of her sorrow and pain.' Her eyes brushed the herd and the First Ones, but she wasn't seeing them.

Taking a deep breath, Candela paused and faced the gathering. She began to speak in almost a whisper.

'I was there when the Book of Divination was first read. I was there when the Staff of the Unimaginable was created from truth, love and all that is good.' She paused and then went on in a louder voice.

'I was there with the very first thoughts that made the Ritual of Return, and I was there when The Circle of Light formed the eleven minor wands.' She looked around the gallery. 'I was there for all of these things.'

Coraggio stepped forward. 'You don't have to do this, wife,' he pleaded, as if he knew her mind like his own.

'We can fight him now, if you need us to!' Oobaat urged.

Hope stepped forward to offer advice.

But Candela faced them and held her ground. 'Number Seven of the First Ones,' she stated, 'is completely mad.' She took a breath. 'But there is always Hope, is there not?' She looked at Hope then, with the question. Hope simply nodded.

Candela continued. 'The Staff of the Unimaginable has just made a cry for help, so, she is not beyond that hope. Perhaps her mind can be swayed back to us, those who love her? This can only be done by a unicorn.' She paused and took another deep breath. Her eyes glittered.

Sudden tears surprised Rielle. More than ever she was struck by Candela's gentle greatness. The tears rested hotly in her throat.

Candela smiled a contradiction to her next words. 'I am going out there. I am going to try to find the white wand and bring her back. If I succeed then it will be much easier to fight the sorcerer, for all of us, in the end.'

Rielle disturbed the hush that followed. 'And if you don't succeed?' she asked, brokenly.

The herd trilled loudly.

Candela glowed. 'If I don't succeed?' she repeated. 'Ah, well, that is something that remains to be seen.' She looked kindly at Rielle. 'There is a destiny here, young Rielle, and no matter what you may think, we are all playing our part in little ways.'

Rielle didn't understand, but this was no time to be questioning a mighty unicorn.

The herd sighed. Candela had chosen her task. They knew that she would not be swayed. Without a word, they gathered around her for the Ritual of Return.

Hope and Oobaat watched patiently as Rielle, Pud and the snails waited cheerlessly in the wings. White light flowed from the Ritual of Return, like a power and a blessing, to encompass everyone.

The ritual tested, Candela stood tall. Then, she strode to the doorway of the tower and briefly paused. The gathering held its breath. Perhaps Candela would change her mind.

Just once, she looked back. 'Destiny we are meeting,' she breathed.

Then, with so much dignity that Rielle finally wept, Candela stepped away from the safety of the tower. She stepped lightly, and alone, into the night, with all the love and power of the herd in her heart.

Rielle hunkered down and held Pud tightly, as if he might leave too.

The Wand of Faith and the Staff of Life began to sing, then, with one solemn voice:

Spirit, Fire, Air, Earth and Water
Moon, Stars, Sun and Sky
We reach out, we reach out
With a summons and a prayer!

CHAPTER 27

Once there was mercy

'The legend of the First Ones is too long to tell here,' Old began, 'so I will tell what I can, to help you understand.'

Will listened, round-eyed, from under his ridiculous hat.

Old looked up from his whittling and stared thoughtfully at him. Will wriggled uncomfortably. As if satisfied with something only he knew, Old proceeded with the tale.

Will leaned forward and sipped more tea.

'When the First Ones were much younger,' Old began, 'The Circle of Light gave to some of us a wooden staff. Each looked like a staff held for walking but we understood they were much more than that. We soon called them, *walking wands*. Not all First Ones were given one of these wands, for there were only eleven of them and there were many more First Ones.'

Old's mouth pulled down at the edges as if the story were somehow disagreeable. He sighed and continued to whittle.

'Unicorns existed long before First Ones. They guarded The Circle of Light and also the Book of Divination. It was through their own wand, the Staff of the Unimaginable, that all the other wands were formed.' He put down his whittling and poured more tea.

Will was impatient. 'Go on,' he urged.

Old nodded and sipped from his cup.

'The Circle of Light gave us the Eleven Wands of Principle.' Old shrugged. 'They are lost now, except for the few we hold, lost some time ago in the battle of the First Ones. Ah, but that is another tale.'

Will shuffled restlessly. 'Tell me about gold,' he urged. 'Why is gold so important, you know, to... to *him*?'

'Wait, you must wait,' Old replied brusquely before going on.

'For many thousands of years, there were all the wands.' Old smiled with memories. 'The wands shared life with us and became, for those who held them, the very core of their being. We held the *Staff of Life*, given to Number One, whom you met as guardian to the wishing pond, long ago. There was the *Wand of Keeping* and the *Wand of Love*, both lost; and the *Wand of Time*.' Old smiled. 'My wand, the one you just briefly held.'

Will rustled, impatiently.

'Be still!' Old barked and Will sat up at attention.

Old resumed his whittling. '*The Staff of Truth*,' he narrated, 'she, too, has gone; as has the *Wand of Beginnings*, the *Staff of Justice*, the *Wand of Endings* and the *Wand of the Unyielding*.'

Will took off his hat and counted on his fingers. 'That's only nine,' he stated. 'That's only nine wands.'

'Wait,' Old growled, 'impatience is not a skill!' He

glared at Will and Will sat still.

'The *Wand of Faith* is held by Enin On, the First One that you call Hope.'

Will nodded, hardly daring to move.

'Good,' Old muttered, 'good.' He sipped his tea then resumed.

'You have seen us, in troubled times, use our walking wands for defence, have you not?'

Will nodded again.

'That is not the purpose of the wands, Will,' Old whispered. 'The wands from The Circle of Light were not made for what you call magic. Oh, no. They were made for the service of First Ones, just as the Staff of the Unimaginable was made to serve Unicorns.'

Will sat taller, intrigued.

Old nodded. 'This *magic,* as you call it, came later, much later, when we had learned much more.' Old sighed and his uncovered eye became a mere slit. 'And then... well, then, there was also the *Wand of Mercy!*'

Will jumped up, forgetting the order to listen and sit.

'You don't mean,' he gasped, 'you can't mean to tell me that the walking wand which belonged to the Sorcerer of Great Contempt... that it was the Wand of Mercy?'

Old sipped more tea for sadness, and blinked solemnly up at Will.

'Indeed,' Old nodded slowly, 'indeed it was.' He gestured. Agitated, Will sat down again.

'But,' Will shook his head, 'how can that be? How could it be?'

Old spoke so quietly that Will held his breath to hear him.

'Number Seven of the First Ones was not always as you know him, Will.'

The night closed in on them and the small fire became a mere pin-prick in the dark. The Wand of Time stopped glowing at her centre.

Will moved closer to hear Old speak.

'Back in the days when First Ones were young, and the wands were new and freshly formed, the mighty unicorns walked easily amongst us. Knowing us as they did, they chose which First Ones to give wands to.' Old shrugged. 'Who would think,' he continued, 'that the mighty unicorns would choose as they did?'

He peered at Will with a raised eyebrow, as if he knew a secret that one day, Will, too, would understand.

'As you know,' Old chuckled, 'they gave to me the Wand of Time. It made no sense. I was young, impatient! I wanted things to happen straight away. I look back to the day I was given this wand and my first thought was that it would be best given to my good brother. My brother was calm and patient; time was already his friend. I did not want this wand at first. I could not understand why I was chosen.' Old looked fondly at the wand on the ground then glanced knowingly at Will.

'I did not choose to be responsible. I was young, busy; but I had no choice. The Book of Divination had been consulted.' With a wry smile he went on.

'The unicorns knew many things. I took the wand, as most who were chosen did, with both a sense of honour and apprehension.'

Old shook his head and sipped more tea.

'You may find this difficult to believe, Will, but it was not so for Neves On. He took the Wand of Mercy with great excitement. He carried the wand with him everywhere and he listened to all the things it had to say. Neves On was honourable in all his tasks. He was fair and even-tempered, believe it or not.'

Will frowned. He fidgeted. He drank some more tea.

'And then many years later,' Old continued, 'maybe several hundreds or thousands, in human time, I cannot remember, Neves On had an argument with a unicorn. It stands clearly in memory, you understand, because to argue with a unicorn does not make sense. A unicorn will not argue unless the other person is at great fault.' Old paused to let his words take effect. He was quiet for so long that Will thought he must have fallen asleep.

Will detested waiting. He scratched his leg. He tapped his foot. He took his hat off and fidgeted with the feather in it. He drummed his fingers, he rubbed his eyes, he yawned, picked his teeth and began to make faces and crack the bones in his hands.

'Enough!' Old barked. 'Show respect!'

Will jumped and bit back a remark. But he resisted the temptation to scratch an insect bite.

'Neves On argued with the unicorn,' Old continued, disbelief at the memory still strong in his voice. 'Soon a crowd of First Ones had gathered to listen. It did not make sense to anyone to argue with a unicorn.' He sipped his tea. 'I remember the unicorn's face. She stood patiently, with sad eyes, even as she tried to reason with him.'

'Sad?' Will asked. 'Why sad?'

Old was unsure how to explain.

'First Ones are not human, Will. They are not unicorns, either. They are somewhere in the middle of both of them.'

Will shook his head, shrugged and leaned forward.

'Alright, First Ones are somewhere in between, I get that bit... but why was the unicorn sad?'

'Because,' Old snapped; 'First Ones should know better than to fight for power!'

Will sat back. 'The sorcerer wanted power? So he was always the same as he is now!'

Old sighed. 'Perhaps, perhaps somewhere within his heart, a grain of vice always stirred. Who knows?' As if to find comfort, Old rested his hand on the Wand of Time. She hummed. Turning back to Will, Old went on.

'Neves On wanted to change the order of things. He wanted the First Ones to have a leader. He wasn't satisfied. He thought he knew a better way than that which had worked perfectly for many thousands of years.'

Will nodded shrewdly. '*He* wanted to be your leader, didn't he?'

'Yes, that he did,' Old replied, 'and no matter how much the unicorn told him it was not necessary to change the order of things, he would not be told.'

Old became silent.

Will thought long and hard. Something stirred in his mind like a distant memory. He knew the answer. He stared at Old in the near-pitch dark.

'The unicorn let him try his way, didn't she?' Will finally offered. 'She let the First Ones pick a leader. Am I right? Then, despite everything, the sorcerer was still not chosen, am I right again?'

Before Old could answer, Will rushed on.

'In his misery at his plan backfiring, he caused the battle of the First Ones, didn't he? Then, finally, when the mayhem and damage was all too much, the unicorns and the remaining First Ones took back the Wand of Mercy and banished him - to this place... *Wish!*'

Old took a deep breath. A shadow crossed his heart. *How much,* Old wondered, *had the sorcerer told Will whilst Will slept?*

'Yes,' he replied, 'that is exactly, in the short version, how events occurred.'

'What about the gold, then?' Will pushed.

Old's face shut down. 'It is enough for you to know that gold is something Neves On must never have!' Old stopped whittling.

Will didn't notice. 'What about the wand he has now, though?' he insisted. 'Isn't it the Wand of Mercy?'

Old held up a hand. 'The wand he holds now Will,' he rumbled, 'is the Staff of the Unimaginable!'

Will sucked in a sharp breath. '*Not* the unicorn wand? How is that possible?'

Old shook his head. He pierced Will with an alarming look.

'It is stolen. He stole the unicorn wand!'

Old stood up abruptly and stepped on the fire to put it out. He turned back to Will. 'Remember,' he whispered, 'that it is never too late to change! Everything, *anything* can always... always, be turned around, mended or repaired! It is never too late to be sorry. It is never too late to change one's ways. I urge you to remember this!'

Will shrunk back. He felt unsure of Old, again. 'What do you mean?' he asked quietly.

The first flickers of a distant dawn gave the orchard a softly lit glow.

Picking up the Wand of Time, Old left the pot and clay mugs where they lay and walked purposefully over to Will.

He lifted one of Will's hands and placed into it the wood he had whittled. Then he turned and walked away.

Will looked down at the small wooden object. The light was just good enough for him to see it well.

'Follow, or not!' Old called as he began to make his way amongst the trees.

Picking his hat up, Will stood to catch up with Old, even as he sent a glance backwards at the dark. He looked again at the wooden object in his hand and touched the statue in wonder. It was an eagle. He looked up. Old's solid back had disappeared.

CHAPTER 28

All things are not done

Candela sensed, rather than heard, the unicorn wand. By the light of the stars, she slipped quietly through the night, treading nimbly amongst the uprooted mass of almond trees. Knowingly, she stopped.

Lying in a pool of green slime, the Staff of the Unimaginable whimpered, even as she still shone white. Quickly, Candela sent the wand a thought. The wand stopped whimpering and lay quietly, as if she were not beyond the truth of kindness.

Leaves flickered. Small creatures chattered. Candela waited. Her horn warned her that evil lurked perilously close by. The night noises faded away. Moments passed. The first faint colour of dawn was stealing, like a delicate pastel jewel, over the tips of the almond trees.

Candela took a deep breath and turned around.

Shattering the charm of dawn like a dark tangible scar, the Sorcerer of Great Contempt, Number Seven of the First Ones, loomed in the clearing.

'Well,' he sneered, 'what have we here? This is not the *little* unicorn coming to us!' He beckoned, and the Staff of the Unimaginable flew, spattered in green slime, into his hand.

'We are graced,' Neves On smirked insolently, 'by a visit from the great Candela, the mother of all unicorns, herself!'

Candela said nothing.

The wand lay silent in the sorcerer's hand as he brushed the slime from her pure white wood.

'Such a pity,' he spat, 'that this wand won't sing for me. Never mind, never mind.' He wiped the last of the slime away. 'I have no need of jingles or poems for I use her for what she's worth.' He turned with a brutal expression to face Candela, as if he dared to rule her.

Candela looked clearly into his livid eyes.

Unbelievably, the sorcerer stepped back and seemed to lose his train of thought. Then anger filled him at Candela's lack of fear. With the white wand held high, he charged at her, but stopped short. Hatred flared from him.

'You!' he glared. 'You dare to challenge me!'

Candela watched him and waited.

The sorcerer turned with a swish of his night-dark cloak, and paced.

'You unicorns never understood me,' he fumed. 'You never tried to understand me. Not even my own kind has ever tried to understand me. *No one has ever understood me!*' He turned with a sneer. 'But I hold the greatest of all wands now, and until I choose to let her go, she is mine to control!'

The wand whimpered in his grasp. He crushed her tightly as if to prove his words.

Candela said nothing.

Neves On faced her with an ugly grin. 'You have made a grave mistake this time,' he laughed, 'for while I hold this wand I can't be conquered by anyone, not by anyone, do you understand? Not for any reason!'

'I have not come to conquer you,' Candela whispered, as white light flowed from her in a steady mist.

The sorcerer looked surprised. 'What do you want, then?' he asked. 'Have you come for a social visit? Or would you like tea and biscuits?' He laughed uncontrollably, amused by his own sarcasm and surly wit.

Candela delivered another thought to the Staff of the Unimaginable.

Remember who made you. Remember that love will always wait for you. Unicorns will always wait for you. Remember the unicorn prayer, remember. Truth will find you, have no fear, you are made by unicorn.

The wand pulsed light from her core. It lasted a fleeting second, but that was enough for Candela. She took a deep breath and waited.

The sorcerer stopped laughing and strode up to Candela. He pushed his sneering face toward her pure white loveliness.

'You have walked straight into my trap, foolish unicorn,' he breathed, 'right into the trap we have set for you!'

Candela focused on the Ritual of Return. She would need it now like never before. The sorcerer turned away.

It was then Candela saw Will standing in the clearing. In one hand Will held an arrow and, in the other, a crossbow.

...

Within the Tower of Dreams, Rielle paced the wide expanse of colourful multi-patterned floors. Anxiously, Pud strode with her. In hushed tones, Oobaat and the herd consulted in the tower's halls.

Rielle heard Hope call out to her; his tone was serious. Rielle stopped pacing and strode into Hope's room.

With wings closed, Far rested on a pile of Hope's books, as if that were the happiest place to be. She waved to Rielle. Rielle smiled briefly.

Hope turned to Rielle. 'There,' he pointed, 'is the golden cake tin that belongs to Number Twenty Three.'

Rielle nodded.

'I want you to know where it is Rielle,' he went on, 'in case something happens to me.'

Rielle flinched. 'Why would something happen to you?'

Far squeaked and flew over to sit on Hope's shoulder.

'Now, now, I didn't say something *would* happen to me, I said in *case* it should!' Hope smiled reassuringly. 'You need to know where it is. After all, it does not belong to me. It belongs to Number Twenty Three, and when he's ready, he shall have it.'

Rielle wondered why Hope was telling her this, but she didn't have a chance to ponder.

Rielle... Rielle... Rielle...

Rielle gasped and looked up at Hope. 'It's that voice calling my name again!'

Surprised, he stared at her from his great height. 'You have a watcher!' he cried.

Rielle gaped at him. 'A watcher? Is that what you call it? All I know is that the voice calls me before something, something…. '

Far squealed but Hope went on. 'Someone watches over you, Rielle,' he stated, 'someone who reaches you in your need!'

'Yes, I suppose so,' Rielle began, 'but I think of it as someone who warns me when something peculiar is going to happen. '

Rielle! Rielle! Rielle!

Outside Hope's chamber, Pud began to wail.

'Pud!' Rielle ran from Hope's room with Hope and Far following at speed.

Oobaat, Coraggio and the herd were gathering together. With one look at Oobaat, Hope understood.

'It is time to leave the safety of this place,' Oobaat commanded. 'It is time to find the path that is ours, and to strive to put an end to evil!'

This time, Hope did not hesitate. 'Forward then!' he called, raising the Wand of Faith. He turned and briefly commanded Rielle and Far. 'Stay here!'

Before Rielle could question him, the unicorns and the First Ones were gone!

Rielle and Far stared at each other. Pud howled once more. As if sharing the same thought, all three of them bolted as fast as they could to the doorway of the tower.

'Stay here?' Rielle bellowed. 'I wouldn't stay here if they tied me to a chair! My friend Old is out there and so is Will, and I will not sit in some cosy room, in some safe place, watching pots boil, while the world threatens to come to an end!'

'Wait for us!' bawled Bibs, as he and little Bobs scuttled to join them.

'Then let's go,' Rielle called.

They all began to run, clattering noisily over the moat's little bridge.

'Do we know where we're going?' Far roared. 'Do we have a clue where to find them?'

Rielle! Rielle! Rielle!

'Hooley bondooley, this is going to be a doozie,' Rielle cried.

'There's someone coming!' called Far. They all turned.

Old galloped through the trees to join them. 'I know where we must go,' he beckoned. 'I know where they have gone. Follow me!'

'Old!' Rielle ran forward with an enormous grin. 'Old, I've missed you. I'm so happy to see you safe!'

Old grinned back at her, as the six of them grouped together and hurtled with a bent of mind that drove them, drove them, as if in their hearts and minds this moment had already happened. Now it was time to make it real.

Just as the sun sent long dwindling shafts of coloured thread to join the almond trees in its morning knitting, Old stopped and pointed.

'There,' he whispered, 'there!'

In a distant clearing, strewn with dead and destroyed trees stood Hope, Oobaat and the unicorn herd.

'Good, we are in time!' Old breathed to Rielle. 'We are in time!'

For one fleeting moment he grasped Rielle's hand in his. He smiled with all the sweetness of his kind being, up into her eyes. Rielle felt her heart stop, as if this was a moment to remember for all time. She smiled back at him, despite the urgency of the moment, and knew he was indeed, her dear, treasured friend.

Then, running again, the small group hurtled at breakneck speed to reach the herd and the First Ones. They stopped beside them. No one looked at them or took any notice. It was as if they hadn't arrived. The herd's silence was so intense that it cut the air like crystal. They were watching something.

Rielle looked to the clearing. At first, the shifting morning light dazzled her eyes, but then she saw what they were seeing.

Will faced Candela across the clearing. In one hand he held an arrow and, in the other, a crossbow. Rielle's heart sank. It couldn't be true! Without thinking, Rielle plunged past the herd and the others.

'No, Will! Stop!' she called.

Like dark oil, the sorcerer turned to Rielle and pinned her with cruel eyes, which glimmered in that moment, with the prospect of his success.

'What have we here?' he sneered. Casting an eye over the unicorn herd and the First Ones, Neves On laughed.

'Get on with it, Will,' he spat, 'or you'll end up being just like this useless lot. Look at them, too afraid to challenge, and only this human girl dares to speak!' He turned his back on all of them.

Rielle stopped in mid run between the herd and the scene unfolding in the clearing. She gasped. There was a rope pulled tightly around Candela's neck. The Sorcerer of Great Contempt held the end of that rope!

Candela waited patiently, her eyes unafraid.

'Remember, Willful James,' Rielle heard Candela whisper, 'you have been blessed. Use your blessings wisely or become like him.' In that moment the sun soared jubilantly to paint the world pink, drenching the clearing with radiance.

Will held the crossbow and the arrow as if, before using them, he would make their acquaintance. He pressed a finger into the arrow tip. It pricked his skin but he didn't feel anything. Then, patiently, he ran his fingers almost lovingly along the wood.

'It's not a wand,' the sorcerer barked. 'No matter how long you become acquainted with it, I promise you, it will not sing!'

'Think carefully, Willful James,' Candela whispered, 'blessings are a powerful thing.'

'Get on with it, Willful James,' Neves On hissed, 'both you and I have somewhere else we'd rather be! You want to go home, and I,' he laughed, 'I am in a hurry to have what is rightfully mine!'

Rielle looked imploringly to the herd and the First Ones. They stood like a solid wall, their faces unreadable.

'Do something!' Rielle pleaded with them. 'Why won't you do something? Do something, please!' Even as she spoke, she felt that there was something that she didn't understand. She turned to Will and stepped forward.

'No, Will! Please, please don't kill her.' Tears poured uselessly down Rielle's face. 'People love you, Will.' Rielle turned and glanced at the unicorns and the First Ones, and then turned back.

'Look at us, Will,' she pleaded, 'we all love you. Please, please don't do this terrible thing! Don't become just like *him!*' She stopped short of looking at the sorcerer as she dared to say it.

As if in a dream, Will examined the crossbow and the arrow. *Such a long time since I held one of these*, he thought.

He looked up. Somewhere in the shadows, sweet Rielle was calling. Tears were pouring down her honest, true face. Will sighed. He knew that he might never see her again. He had told her all his secrets and she had still remained his friend. His eyes flicked to the sorcerer and then, for the first time, he noticed the herd. Hope, Oobaat and Old also stood by.

Will locked eyes with Old.

In his pocket, Will could feel the small wooden eagle that Old had whittled for him. His heart warmed toward the First One. He thought how nice it might have been to get to know him better. Apart from Rielle, Old had taken the time to be his friend.

As Old held his gaze, Will smiled briefly. *Goodbye,* Will thought.

The sorcerer loomed into Will's mind. *'Get on with it! Get on with it, Willful James! Kill her, kill her now!'*

Will raised the bow. It was aimed perfectly at Candela.

Coraggio began to course forward to take the arrow for her instead, but Oobaat stopped him.

'Wait!' insisted Number One of the First Ones. 'Wait!'

Will fixed his sight. He knew he must not miss the mark he sought.

The world stood frozen with terror in its throat.

Rielle turned away and fell to her knees. Pud ran to her and she held him hard. He whined and licked her face.

With a twang, the arrow hurtled through the air, and with an aim that was truly perfect, it sliced the noose from Candela's neck!

Will dropped his arms and closed his eyes. *I did it!* He thought. *I got it right!* Sweat dripped from his forehead. His body trembled and his hands shook.

Number Seven of the First Ones gaped with malevolent disbelief. Darkness oozed and spread through the air around him.

Rielle began to run forward, to tell Will how wonderful he was, but Will held up a hand. The way he did it stopped her sharply in her tracks.

'Go, Candela,' Will urged, 'go back to your herd where you belong.'

Will turned then, and deliberately faced the sorcerer. He flung the crossbow at Neves On's feet.

I will die now, Will thought.

The unicorns merged to engulf Candela; the Ritual of Return was pouring like a river.

Oobaat, Hope and Old stood their ground with their walking wands held ready. The air in the orchard crackled.

The sorcerer stepped toward Will. Will held his gaze. The dark haze surrounding Neves On deepened. He was speechless with fury and disbelief. Speechless that a mere human, the *same* mere human, had disobeyed him again! He seethed into the fragile morning.

Swiftly, Oobaat, Hope and Old exchanged thoughts.

The young man was no match for Neves On, not ever, but especially not now that the boy had disobeyed him.

'It's time!' Oobaat sent the thought to Hope and Old.

'*Yes, Number One of the First Ones, we are called now to fight.*'

As one, they stepped forward.

Old glanced at Rielle who still stood half-way toward the clearing. His heart went out to her tear-streaked face. He pulled his eye-patch over his head and beckoned her to him. She ran gratefully to his side.

'You might take care of this for me, dear Rielle,' Old smiled. 'I need to see with all of me now.' As he handed the eye-patch to her, his soft, doeskin hands brushed hers.

Rielle took the eye-patch. She wanted to say something - something that would make this day right. But the words stuck in her throat.

'Go now,' Old urged, 'leave this place, and take the others with you!'

Oobaat called out to Will. 'Will, you did well.'

Will ignored him. His eyes were still locked with the sorcerer's.

Self-loathing crawled on Will's skin. Because of him, everyone there was now in danger. He took a step toward the sorcerer, who was sneering at him and preparing Will's fate.

A swift thought passed between Oobaat, Hope and Old. That was enough for Oobaat. Rushing to Will, he pushed him with a mighty shove, flinging Will from the path of peril.

In that moment the world went mad. With a scream to stop the sun, the sorcerer raised the Staff of the

Unimaginable and turned to face his brothers.

Hope, Oobaat and Old raised their wands with one action.

'Now!' Oobaat boomed. 'Now!'

The three wands of the First Ones came together to block the searing terror flung from the Staff of the Unimaginable.

Behind them the unicorns stood like a solid wall and coursed dynamic light to join the battle.

Once again, Number Seven of the First Ones commanded the wand he held, and once again, she sent scorching power through the air.

The three minor wands took the blow, but they could not do this forever.

'Deflect, send it back to him!' Oobaat breathed.

With the next onslaught from the sorcerer, the three minor wands used all their might with the authority of their wielders, to send the terror straight back to him.

The sorcerer had underestimated his brothers. Their ploy worked. The Staff of the Unimaginable was flung from his hand, and the sorcerer was pitched, injured, to the ground.

Neves On lay stunned for only moments, but in those moments, Hope ran to pick up the unicorn wand, securing his own wand beneath one arm.

Smoke and stench filled the clearing. It darkened the air, despite the sun, which had now fully risen, striving to shine golden.

Triumphantly, Hope reached the Staff of the Unimaginable and grasped her with both hands.

Threatened and provoked, the sorcerer found new vigour and flung molten fire to destroy Hope.

Rielle watched through a cloud of dirt and smoke, as she clung to Pud at the edge of the clearing.

Oobaat and Old used their wands to block the fireball. Hope was still safe!

Desperate to win, crazed with the need for victory and unable to accept defeat, the sorcerer no longer cared what he did. Even as he grovelled, wounded, on the ground, he sent a fireball to the Staff of the Unimaginable *herself.* It hit her!

The herd gasped. Everyone watched in disbelief.

The Staff of the Unimaginable flooded a shriek into the morning. The sound stabbed the unicorns to their hearts.

Hope reeled, gasping. Holding the white wand, the bolt from the fireball stunned him to his core. If not for a broken log in his path, he would have fallen, razed, to the ground. Tenaciously, he clasped the Staff of the Unimaginable in his hands. Juddering inwardly, he strove for breath. His strength convulsed and his life-force trembled. But Hope had only one thought. *The white wand must be returned to unicorns!*

'Let go!' Oobaat boomed. 'Let go, or it will kill you, Hope!'

Hope held on. He strove to use the power from his own wand, the Wand of Faith, to stave off the attack, but no minor wand could do so much.

Horrified, Rielle stood up. She watched as Hope began to die. She turned. Will had come to stand beside her. Sobbing, she flung herself into Will's arms. Helplessly, Will held her.

And so it was that Will clearly saw what happened

next, and Rielle did not. So clearly did he see it that it would stay with him, night and day, for evermore.

Smiling, almost secretly, Old stepped up to the dying Hope. With a mighty shove, he pushed Hope as hard as he could. Hope stumbled weakly, and in doing so, Old snatched the Staff of the Unimaginable, grasping her firmly.

'No!' Hope called, as life came back to him. 'No!'

Old looked serenely into his brother's eyes. 'The world needs Hope,' is all he said.

The Staff of the Unimaginable could not stop the power of the poison that had been seared into her. The fireball inside her coruscated a warning, and then exploded outward with terrifying force.

Old was flung onto the ground, and the Staff of the Unimaginable was catapulted through the air like a spinning missile, to lie lost from sight.

Oobaat turned furiously to the place where the Sorcerer of Great Contempt had fallen to the ground. Against the laws of First Ones and unicorns, he held the Staff of Life high and called, 'End! Be no more!'

But the sorcerer had disappeared. Only his black cloak lay, like a dishevelled curse, upon the ground.

CHAPTER 29

Our day will come

Rielle turned around. The smoke was clearing. The unicorn herd was gathered around something that she couldn't see.

'We have tried our best,' she heard Coraggio say, 'but not even the Ritual of Return can heal these wounds.'

Rielle looked at Will, puzzled. *Hope was standing there. He had survived! What did Coraggio mean?*

Will looked dazed; he just shook his head.

Rielle felt something tap her leg. She looked down. Bibs and little Bobs looked up at her.

'It's Old,' Bibs whispered. Little Bobs nodded, round-eyed.

'Old?' Rielle repeated. She looked over at the unicorns. 'Old!' she cried, running as fast as she could toward the herd. Pud galloped after her. Together they pushed their way to the centre of the gathered unicorns.

Old lay with a smile on his half-moon mouth and the Wand of Time held in one hand.

'Old?' Rielle quivered. 'Are you alright?'

Old beckoned to her. Rielle knelt down.

'Dear Rielle,' he whispered, 'I have words to share with you.' He took one of her hands in his free one. 'Promise me,' he said, 'that you will do these things.'

Rielle nodded even before she heard what he had to say.

Old smiled at her. 'Through all your days, open your heart and let life in, otherwise, the one we hurt most is ourselves. Don't walk through life with fear, doubt or guilt. Don't hide; let your heart shine through. Be free to live, love and be true.'

Rielle nodded again.

Old looked up past her. Will was standing there. Rielle wondered if the words were meant mostly for her or for Will, or perhaps for both of them, because they were humans.

Old paused and gathered his breath. He looked at Rielle again and squeezed her hand.

'You set me free, young Rielle. When you fell into my mountain cave, you gave me reason to go outside again.'

Rielle squeezed his hand back. She couldn't speak. Old was a First One and they lived for thousands and thousands of years, so surely he'd be alright, wouldn't he?

Old kept Rielle's small hand in his.

'Willful James,' Old murmured and gestured.

Will kneeled, his face a wretched map of guilt. 'I'm sorry,' he pleaded, 'all this is my fault. It should be me lying there!'

Old smiled sweetly. 'Be still,' he breathed, 'remember you would be a prince and a warrior. No feeling sorry for yourself!'

Will started to get up and leave.

'Stay, Will,' Old barked. Carefully then, as if strength

were leaving him fast, Old gently let Rielle's hand go. Feebly, he lifted the Wand of Time. He gestured for Will to take her.

Will looked down at his own hands. 'I can't take her,' he gasped. 'I've just held a bow and arrow. I'm not worthy to mind this wand for you. It might be best if you let someone else have her.'

'She is yours to wield now, Willful James,' Old whispered, 'but remember, be careful how you use her.'

'I can't *take* the wand!' Will protested, white-faced. 'I'm not even a First One!'

Old made a face to silence him. 'The Wand of Time is not the greatest of them all,' he whispered, 'but you must know this one important thing: *Things you make they cannot break, when you hold the Wand of Time!*'

With the little strength he had left, Eerht Ytnewt On, Number Twenty Three of the First Ones, took Rielle's hand back into one of his, softer than doe hair as it was. With the other hand, he raised the Wand of Time and held her to his cheek. Then he handed the wand, with purpose, to Will.

Will peered around, embarrassed. Reluctantly, he took the wand. 'I am not worthy,' he cried.

Old looked up at Will with both eyes, and smiled kindly at him. 'You are more than worthy, my friend. You have more worth than you believe.'

'I… I am the cause of all of this!' Will looked around at the devastated forest and then at Old himself. 'How can you give me a wand made for First Ones?'

Old stirred slightly. 'We are the same,' he whispered.

259

'You are as I was, and I am as you will be.'

'I'm nothing like you!' Will gasped. 'You're just, and wise and kind and brave and I'm... I'm nothing like you!'

Old smiled and chuckled. 'Why do you think I let you take the wand by the fire, Will?' Will shook his head. 'Because,' Old breathed, 'we are like two sides of the same coin, my friend.'

'Then why do you have to die?' Will grieved. 'I need to learn from you. We all need you. We... we can't go on without you, Old!'

Old sighed. 'Everything you need to know from me, Will, I have already taught you.' He paused. 'You can go home one day, Willful James, if you choose. *But not until you finish what it is you started!*'

Old turned to Rielle again and beamed broadly at her.

'A goozey boozey,' he whispered, 'is a dear and treasured one... who is obvious and yet mysterious, amusing and yet exasperating, and very interesting to know. That is a goozey boozey!' And, so saying, Old placed a small packet of something into her hand.

Rielle looked down. 'Tea for sadness,' she whispered, and despite her anguish, she tried to smile.

Old closed his eyes then. He gave one last sigh, and the spirit within him rose up in the shape of an eagle. The eagle sang as it soared:

Don't be sad
Don't be sad
Nothing ever lasts forever
But nothing ever ends.

The eagle flew into the sky until they could no longer see it.

Old left Will and Rielle, and all the others who had known him, richer than they had ever been, yet feeling poorer than they had ever thought possible.

Gently, Rielle held Old's doeskin hand one last time. 'I love you Old,' she whispered, 'you were my dear friend.'

Pud howled then, as was his habit, when things were just too much to bear.

Benny walked to Rielle's side as Candela and Coraggio stood reverently by. The herd hung their heads. They knew that Old was safe, but it pained them to see the sadness of the humans.

'Come, Rielle,' Benny murmured, 'come away. Give Will some time alone.'

Rielle looked with gratitude at the little unicorn. He had never failed her, not ever, not once. She placed Old's beloved hand back on his chest, and with a last look at him, she turned away. Benny and the herd closed around her and covered her with light.

'I could really use some tea for sadness now,' Rielle choked, before bursting into heartrending sobs.

Will still kneeled beside Old. The wand in his hand felt vaguely familiar from the time at the fireside when Old had let him hold her.

'She needs to sing for you once more,' he choked. Lifting one of Old's hands while it was still warm, he brushed the wand with it so she would sing. But the Wand of Time had a new master now, and that master was Will. She stayed silent.

'Then I will ask her to sing for you,' Will whispered defiantly. Feeling like an impostor, Will held the wand in both hands like an offering.

'Sing,' he pleaded, almost as a question, 'please sing once more for our great, good friend.'

The unicorns and the others held their breath. Would the wand accept him, as Old had hoped? For long, trying moments, time skipped and hopped like a heart beat.

Then, just as Will felt tears in his throat, the Wand of Time began to hum and then her voice soared in freedom:

Spirit, Fire, Air, Earth and Water
Moon, Stars, Sun and Sky

The Truth of Time we have been seeking
Destiny we are now meeting

Mastery is not in keeping
It comes not from hands but from hearts

It comes from knowing
Understanding, at last.

Before he even knew he had done it, Will held the Wand of Time against his cheek, just as he had seen Old do.

'Thank you,' he whispered, honoured. 'Thank you!' And then he turned at last to Rielle and the others.

CHAPTER 30

Wish Again

Benny and the herd searched the clearing. No matter how hard they looked, they could not find where the Staff of the Unimaginable had landed. She was gone, as was the Sorcerer of Great Contempt.

'We failed,' Will whispered. Holding the Wand of Time carefully as if he still couldn't believe that she was now his, he held back a wave of grief.

'No, no, we didn't fail.' Hope put a hand on his shoulder and turned Will to look at him. 'Did you think that it would be so easy, Willful James? Did you really believe that one battle would be enough to foil his evil?'

Will looked at Hope with held-back tears.

'I hoped it would be,' he replied. 'I wanted it to be enough. This whole business has gone on already, for too long. It's my fault, isn't it? I started it all long ago with my stupid, thoughtless wishes and my careless, selfish ways!'

Hope shook his head. 'You were merely a pawn in his game, a tool for him to use, Will, that's all.' Hope sighed. 'Neves On was trouble long, long before you were even a thought, let alone born.'

Will shook Hope off. 'No,' he insisted, 'I can't help believing that, in my own way, I have made his evil worse.' Will glared at Hope and Oobaat as they watched him kindly. It made him hate himself even more.

Why were they so good to him? Why had Old been so very good to him? Why was everyone so patient and forbearing and kind, despite his weakness and the past he dragged around, no matter how hard he tried to shake it off?

Will sighed, watching the unicorns as they searched painstakingly for their wand: the wand that wasn't there, just as the sorcerer wasn't there. He shrunk from the black, forbidding cloak that lay crumpled and tarnished on the ground; the cloak that the sorcerer had left behind.

What fate, now, for all of them? Should they pursue him? Or leave the fight for another day?

'If I could wish again,' Will breathed, glancing at the First Ones, 'then I would change it all, right from the start.' He looked at Rielle and Pud and the snails, with their tear stains and sad, patient faces and wondered why they didn't hate him. 'But I have made my bed,' he groaned, almost to himself, 'and now I hold the Wand of Time.' Will's voice cracked, before he quickly recovered. 'As Old said... I must finish what I started.'

Hope and Oobaat nodded. Without another word, they went to where Old lay. They glanced at each other, then covered Old's body with light from their walking wands, and made it disappear. They turned to Will and Rielle who watched on, wide-eyed.

'First Ones do not have human-style burials,' Hope politely explained.

Rielle nodded. It seemed like a good way to do things.

The herd stopped looking for the Staff of the Unimaginable and returned to stand with the others.

'She's gone,' Coraggio stated, 'and so the story is not over yet.'

'The white wand will come back to us,' Oobaat breathed. 'We just need to find another way.'

'There's something we haven't thought of yet,' Benny agreed. 'There will be a way of stopping the sorcerer's treacherous ways. We'll find a way to bring our wand home.'

'First let us recover from *this* fight,' Candela urged. 'The humans need rest.'

'Number Seven has gone to ground in any case,' Oobaat growled. 'Who knows how badly he was hurt? Who knows when he will return?'

'Or whether he will return?' Will asked, hopefully.

Both Oobaat and Hope turned to him.

'Oh have no doubt, young man,' Oobaat began...

'He will return... he will return,' Hope concluded.

Will flinched. Pulling his ridiculous hat down low on his head, he muttered, 'Well, I have to go now.' He intended to escape, to make his own way, to leave the unicorns and First Ones and his memories behind. He turned to walk away but his eye caught Rielle standing there, looking lost and uncertain.

Far flew out from where she had been hiding to land on Rielle's shoulder. Rielle smiled wanly. She reached a hand to Pud. He nudged her and pushed into her leg.

'Yes, I have to go too,' Rielle murmured wistfully. 'I must go on to find my dream.'

Bibs and little Bobs took their places by her side. 'We want to stick with you,' Bibs said. Little Bobs nodded in agreement.

Will sighed. Pointing down an avenue of dishevelled trees, he asked, 'Are you going that way, Rielle?'

Rielle nodded. 'Yes,' she replied, 'I think I am.'

'We're all going that way,' Benny stated loudly. 'Aren't we?'

The herd trilled, and the First Ones nodded.

Trotting beside his beloved mistress, faithful Pud nudged her again and then gazed up at her with a broad dog's grin.

Rielle patted him and her heart swelled. Briefly, her memory stirred. A quick picture of Pud walking beside Old came into her mind just as a bird cried loudly overhead. Rielle looked up. High above them an eagle circled.

Looking down again, Rielle's eyes rested on the clearing. The dust and the smoke had settled and the ruined trees seemed almost peaceful in the morning sun. Rielle glanced to where the sorcerer's black cloak had lain. Perhaps it was a trick of the light, but the cloak was gone.

With a deep breath, Rielle turned to the way ahead. For no reason that she could understand, the unicorn herd, each and every one of them, suddenly called, richly, longingly and hauntingly. The sound filled the almond orchard until all her senses reeled. Rielle looked back once more at the clearing, and her heart skipped a beat. As if by magic, the ruined orchard was restored!

Wish

Wish Again

The Third Wish

Hope

Journey of Trees

About the Author

Deby Adair is a writer and artist. She loves all animals and believes we must take care of our natural world.

UnicornKisses®

www.ingramcontent.com/pod-product-compliance
Lightning Source LLC
Chambersburg PA
CBHW030635110726
47901CB00002B/459

Cover image: Jimmy Bay on Unsplash.

ISBN-13: 978-0-6482523-1-3

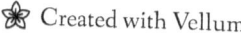 Created with Vellum